"I never had any luck with courting."

Grace glanced up at Aaron as she offered a sincere grin. "I know the right woman for you is out there, Aaron. You're too caring and kind to be a bachelor forever."

Aaron started to respond, but one look at Grace's dazzling eyes took his breath away. He faked a cough in hopes that she wouldn't notice his flustered state, and in doing so, he inhaled one of the dandelion seeds that was floating past. He choked and sputtered before finally spitting the fuzzy seed out.

Having witnessed the ordeal, Grace burst out into peals of laughter.

Aaron couldn't help but give in to his own fit of chuckles. If anyone else had caught him in such a state, he'd have assumed they were laughing at him. Yet Grace had a way of putting him at ease. It was just one more thing that endeared him to her. He wasn't ready to make his move just yet, but he could be putting his heart on the line sooner rather than later.

T0112720

Risking Her
Amish Heart

JACKIE STEF

LOVE INSPIRED

INSPIRATIONAL ROMANCE

LOVE INSPIRED®
INSPIRATIONAL ROMANCE

Recycling programs for this product may not exist in your area.

ISBN-13: 978-1-335-93665-3

Risking Her Amish Heart

Love Inspired
22 Adelaide St. West, 41st Floor
Toronto, Ontario M5H 4E3, Canada
www.LoveInspired.com

Printed in Lithuania

MIX
Paper | Supporting
responsible forestry
FSC® C021394

I can do all things through Christ
which strengtheneth me.
—*Philippians* 4:13

This book is dedicated to Shelby Romanowski, Mekaelah Moray and Angel Milazzo, three very special friends who helped me figure out Grace and Aaron's love story. A special thank-you also to Diane Stefanowicz for her endless support.

Chapter One

"*Daadi*? Are you home?"

Grace Ebersol had just arrived at her grandfather's stone cottage with her suitcase in hand. It was a hot, humid July day in the village of Bird-in-Hand, Pennsylvania, and she was eager to get out of the sun. A gust of earthy-scented air whipped around her, causing the ribbons of her heart-shaped *kapp* to flap against her face. Perhaps a thunderstorm was brewing, and for sure and for certain, the local farmers were praying for rain.

Summertime in Lancaster County normally brought twenty-three-year-old Grace endless amounts of pleasure. She adored the special time of year when sunflowers and cornstalks stood tall and proud. She enjoyed the sight of gardens bursting with homegrown produce and watching lightning bugs twinkle above fields of soybeans, alfalfa, and golden wheat once night blanketed the quiet countryside. She also usually looked forward to the times when she joined her unmarried peers for picnics, volleyball games, and work frolics.

However, this year Grace couldn't muster the slightest bit of enthusiasm for all that summer had to offer, not when her heart had been broken and her world turned upside down.

Keep it together. Daadi *needs you, so you have to stay strong.*

Grace exhaled forcefully to keep her emotions from bubbling over. She couldn't focus on her sorrow now, not when she'd come to cook and keep house for her elderly grandfather.

Daadi Eli was nearing his eighty-first birthday and until recently, he'd been as nimble as a man who was one-fourth of his age. After losing his wife, *Grossmammi* Katie, five years ago, Eli had started physically slowing down. He continued to run his custom furniture-making business from the woodshop that was located only a few dozen rooster steps away from the cottage, though Grace wondered how much longer he would be able to keep up that pace.

Grace knocked again and pressed her ear on the door, then listened for any movement on the other side. When she didn't hear a peep, she tried the doorknob and found that the door was unlocked.

She was pleased to see that things were tidy when she stepped into the small kitchen. Some of her siblings and cousins had been taking turns looking in on rapidly aging Eli, but now it would be Grace's role to care for her grandfather and his cottage. Grace was tenderhearted, cared deeply for others, and eagerly volunteered to come to her *Daadi*'s aid. Cooking, cleaning, and providing companionship for her good-natured grandfather would be a pleasure. She'd be staying here in Bird-in-Hand until a *daadi haus* could be built onto her father's farmhouse for Eli to move into, though she hoped that project would take longer than expected, allowing her to enjoy the change of pace and scenery for as long as possible.

Hopefully keeping busy will provide a decent distraction. Goodness knows that I've been dwelling on my pain for far too long, Grace thought as she placed her suitcase on the shining linoleum floor. Her soul craved a respite from the constant gloom that she just couldn't shake. Memories of happier times plagued her like a stubborn cold that one just couldn't get over, no matter how much chicken soup they consumed.

Grace hurried across the kitchen to search the other rooms for *Daadi* but paused when she noticed a yellow legal tablet on the small kitchen table. A note had been written in unsteady handwriting.

"*Wilkumme*, Gracie. *Denki* for coming to help your *alt Daadi*. I'll be in the woodshop when you arrive. Take your time settling in, and I'll look forward to catching up with you at suppertime. Love, *Daadi*."

She grinned, imagining her grandfather's warm voice as her turquoise eyes scanned the note. Satisfied that everything was just as it should be, she picked up her suitcase and made her way through the cottage to the spare bedroom.

The familiar room was just as quaint and inviting as she remembered it to be. It was small, though it had two large windows that let in plenty of light as well as provided a magnificent view of Mill Creek, the gentle stream that separated *Daadi*'s property from the neighboring farm. A lovely pink, purple, and white quilt stitched in a wedding ring pattern adorned the bed, which had undoubtedly been sewn by *Grossmammi* Katie. The room didn't have a closet, but it was home to a large oak dresser that had been expertly handcrafted by *Daadi* himself, and that was worth more than two closets to Grace.

Deciding to make herself at home, Grace hefted her suitcase onto the bed and undid the latch. She unpacked her clothing, grooming items, stationery, journal, cross-stitching supplies, and well-loved Bible. When everything was neatly stowed away in its proper place, she sat on the bed and surveyed the room. It was simply decorated to the extent that any Amish bedroom would be, yet it felt empty.

She let out a long sigh, knowing that it wasn't the room that was truly empty.

Grace Ebersol and Ben Zook had been close childhood friends, and their friendship had developed into something more by the time they reached their teenage years. Grace had fallen deeply in love with her beau and had every reason to believe that he had the same feelings for her. As time went on and Grace watched many of her female friends tie the knot, she'd told herself that it wouldn't be long until it was her turn to be a bride. She was starting to feel impatient but decided to wait for Ben's proposal. After all, he was the love of her life, and love was worth the wait.

A lot of good that decision did for me. Grace groaned inwardly as she recalled the night that Ben had suddenly broken off their relationship and promptly left their Amish community in one swift move. The unexpected loss of her beau and childhood friend to the outside world felt like a slap in the face, and the sting of that slap never seemed to lessen over time. Nearly eight months had passed since the incident that had turned her world upside down, yet the wound still felt fresh.

Eight months of heartbreak. Eight months of people pestering me to move on, Grace thought as she wiped her teary eyes on the hem of her black apron. Her friends and family urged her to look on the bright side and consider giving love another chance, insisting that plenty of decent fish were in the sea. After the initial sting of her grief had passed, Grace slowly resumed seeking small moments of joy in her daily life. However, she would not allow herself to be tricked by another man into a meaningless courtship ever again. Her heart had been shattered once, and once was enough.

The sound of squeaking door hinges echoed from the other end of the cottage. *Daadi* must've come in to see if she'd arrived. Knowing that she looked a sight from her brief emotional spell, Grace took a moment to compose herself before exiting the bedroom.

As she made her way down the short hallway, Grace heard the gas-powered refrigerator door open, the glass milk bottles it held gently clanging together from the movement.

"*Daadi*? Are you *hungerich*? Would you like me to make you something to eat?" Grace asked as she rounded the corner before letting out a shrill gasp.

A young Amish man whom she didn't recognize stood near the kitchen counter, pouring something into one of two large thermoses. Though he was tall and muscular, he flinched at her gasp like a startled fawn. His blue shirt and black trousers were both covered in sawdust, and a few wood shavings clung to his unruly golden-brown hair.

They stared at each other for several long seconds, both frozen in place.

"I'm just getting some meadow tea," the man finally said as he began filling the second thermos.

"I can see that!" Grace let out a huff. "I think you may have the wrong *haus*."

The man shook his head, causing several wood shavings to flutter down to the floor. "*Nee*, I work with Eli out in the woodshop. Just came in to refill our cups."

Grace's hand flew to her chest. "I guess that's why you're so dusty." She took a deep breath then exhaled, allowing her heart rate to slow. "You really startled me."

"Sorry about that," he gruffly responded.

"*Ach*, no harm done."

Grace offered him a friendly smile but the young fellow immediately dropped his gaze to the floor.

"My name is Grace Ebersol. I'm one of Eli's *kinnskind*." She stepped forward and held out her hand.

"Aaron King," the man replied, with a small grin that looked more like a grimace. He accepted her hand and gave it a quick, half-hearted shake before placing the plastic pitcher of tea back in the refrigerator.

"It's *gut* to meet you," Grace replied, feeling some gritty sawdust on her palm. She inconspicuously wiped her hand on the back of her plum-colored dress. "I live over in Paradise, but I'll be staying here with *Daadi* for a while."

She expected Aaron to comment or ask a question, but he remained silent. Was there something that he didn't like about her? Maybe he was just having a bad day and didn't feel like chatting.

Grace kept her winning smile and pressed on. "Can I get you and *Daadi* something to eat? I'd be glad to make some sandwiches and bring them to the shop."

"*Nee*, *denki*," Aaron answered so quietly that Grace was barely able to make out what he'd said. He secured the lids of both thermoses, took one in each hand, and headed for the door.

Grace followed after him. "Are you sure? Maybe you'd like some…"

"Not now, *denki*." Cradling one of the thermoses in the crook of his arm, he reached for the doorknob and stepped outside. "See you later." As he closed the door behind him without waiting for Grace to reply, several more wood shavings fell out of his hair and clothing, leaving a mess on the floor.

Grace stood motionless, her hands on her hips and her mouth hanging open. She'd never met such a blunt, awkward fellow. Not only had he been short with her, but he'd also left a trail of wood shavings through the kitchen for her to clean up.

First my former beau, and now Aaron King. One inconsiderate man left my life and now another one shows up, Grace grumbled to herself, groaning inwardly as she went in search of a broom and dustpan.

Well, that could have gone better, Aaron King huffed to himself as he plodded back to Eli Ebersol's woodshop and kicked at a small stone that lay in his path. Ever since his childhood days, Aaron had been the shy, awkward type. As a young boy, he'd hoped that he'd develop a strong sense of self-confidence by the time he reached his teenage years, but that didn't happen. Even now, just after his twenty-fifth birthday, Aaron remained just as bashful and uncertain as he had been in his youth. He felt like a bumbling fool when interacting with someone he didn't know well, and that feeling was magnified when in the presence of a beautiful woman.

Grace Ebersol was the definition of natural beauty, with her ebony hair, spattering of freckles, and the bluest eyes that Aaron had ever seen. More importantly, she seemed kindhearted and friendly, just like her grandfather.

I wish Eli would have given me a heads-up that he had company, Aaron thought as he passed through the woodshop's storm door. *Maybe I could have made a better first impression if we hadn't startled each other.*

Aaron walked across the woodshop and inhaled the scent of lumber and wood stain, two familiar odors that brought him comfort. He'd worked for Ebersol's Country Furniture for nearly five years, after working several years for a Mennonite construction company. He loved being able to turn a few pieces of wood into a hope chest, rocking chair, or dining table, and he took great care in crafting the finest pieces under Eli's tutelage. Plus, Eli always greeted and assisted customers, meaning Aaron could stay behind the scenes in the workshop, where he was most comfortable.

Aaron found Eli brushing cherry-colored stain onto a rocking chair that he had finished sanding earlier that day. The old man's brushstrokes were somewhat shaky, so Eli made sure to go over bits where the bristles had previously missed.

"Here's your cold tea," Aaron said as he handed his employer one of the thermoses, holding it firmly until he was sure that Eli had a steady grasp on the cup.

Eli grinned and took a sip of the chilled meadow tea. "*Denki.* I needed something to wet my whistle." He took another long sip before slowly placing the thermos on a nearby workbench. "You didn't happen to run into my *kinnskind,* Gracie, did ya?"

Aaron placed his thermos next to Eli's. "*Jah,* she was in the *haus.* We scared each other half to death."

Eli's eyes brightened behind his thick glasses. "*Gut,* I'm glad she made it here safely. She hired a driver to get here, and I always worry about folks riding in *maschien*, going way too fast for my liking."

Aaron nodded, understanding Eli's concerns. He picked up a paintbrush, dipped it into the can, and began applying even coats of stain on the back of the rocking chair, focusing first on the six spokes of the backrest.

"Gracie's from Paradise, where most of my *familye* live," Eli went on as he picked up his brush and resumed staining the front of the chair. "Her *daed* and *brieder* are working on building a *daadi haus* onto their place for me, which I'll be moving into as soon as it's completed."

Aaron looked up from his work and stared at his employer, wondering if he'd heard that correctly. A buggy ride from Paradise to Bird-in-Hand was long and inconvenient to take daily, and hiring a driver to bring him to and from the woodshop would soon become expensive. He hoped Eli wasn't thinking of moving the business to Paradise or shutting it down altogether. It would be disheartening to lose a job that he enjoyed so much.

"If it's not overstepping my place, I'm wondering what you plan to do with the business," Aaron quietly voiced, keeping his eyes trained on the spokes as he went back to brushing on the stain.

Eli chortled then coughed. "Worried about your job?"

"A little," Aaron replied, feeling his face grow warm.

"*Ach*, no need to be," Eli said, his voice full of familiar reassurance. "I've been thinking of the best time for us to have this conversation, but now that Gracie is here, the cat's nearly out of the bag." He waited for Aaron to look him in the eye. "I'm getting too *alt* to keep up with the demands of the woodshop, and I'd like to pass on the business to you, with a few conditions."

"What?" Aaron exclaimed, dropping his paintbrush. He caught it before it hit the dusty floor, but covered his hands with stain in the process.

Eli chuckled as he rose from his seat. "You're a fine *yung* craftsman, and I can't think of anyone I'd rather pass along my business to." He shuffled over to a cardboard box that was filled with clean rags, selected one, and tossed the cloth to Aaron.

Aaron caught the rag and wiped the sticky liquid from his hands. "Are you sure about this? Wouldn't you rather pass on the business to one of your *kinner* or *kinnskind*?"

Eli lowered himself onto the squeaky stool beside the workbench. "I considered that, but the younger generation is keen on dairy farming. My sons both inherited farms from their wives' *familye*, and their sons want to partner in those operations, except for one who is apprenticing as a blacksmith." Eli smiled, causing his deep wrinkles to swallow his features. "You show great interest in carpentry and even greater skill."

"I… I don't have enough money saved up to buy the business from you," Aaron admitted, using his financial state to cover up his feelings of inadequacy.

Eli waved his gnarled hand through the air, brushing away Aaron's excuse. "I'm not looking to make a profit. I just want to retire and pass along Ebersol's Country Furniture into capable hands, hands that would run the place just as I would."

Though he didn't believe himself capable of running such a successful business, Aaron felt honored that Eli thought so highly of him. "W-what are the conditions you mentioned earlier?"

"I'm glad you asked," Eli said with what almost sounded

like relief. "You will be completely in charge of things around here as of right now. I'll watch as you talk with customers, order supplies, and keep up with the book-keeping. You need to prove to yourself, and to me, that you have the confidence to run the woodshop. If you can't prove this, I'll have to ask someone else to take over for me, and I'd like to avoid that, if possible."

Aaron couldn't believe what he was hearing. He'd always dreamed of owning a carpentry shop, but he'd thought it nothing more than a pipe dream. He knew he lacked the self-assurance it would take to make important decisions, and due to his shyness, he lacked the people skills he'd need to interact with customers. Yet if he didn't force himself to step up to the plate, he'd miss out on this opportunity, one that any young carpenter would jump at.

"*Denki* for believing in me, Eli. I think you're the first person who ever has," Aaron finally said after several minutes of internal debate. "I'd be honored to take over the business when you're ready to retire."

"*Gut*, that's just what I wanted to hear," Eli cheered, offering his unsteady hand to Aaron.

They shook hands and the deal was sealed.

Aaron was completely overwhelmed by Eli's gener-osity, and for the first time in ages, he felt excited about the future.

"There's one more thing I'd like to discuss," Eli added as he peeked over his shoulder and scanned the workshop. "I have a small favor to ask."

Aaron had resumed staining the rocking chair, more eager than ever to please his boss. "I'll be *froh* to help in any way that I can," he said with sincerity, willing to go out of his way to help Eli after the man had acted so selflessly.

Eli looked around the shop once more as if to make sure they were alone. "What did you think of my Gracie when you met her?"

Aaron felt some perspiration gather on his forehead. The way that Eli lowered his voice and asked such a direct question made him uneasy. The first thing he'd noticed about Grace was her beauty. Even in her plain Amish dress and apron, she was as lovely as the first flowers of spring after a bone-chilling winter.

"She seems nice," Aaron finally replied without looking up from his work.

"*Ach*, she is. She's as sweet as a sticky bun, and you won't meet anyone with a gentler heart." Eli took off his straw hat and ran his fingers through his thin, gray hair. "Gracie's had a rough few months, and it worries our *familye* to see her so glum. She does her best to hide her sadness, but I can tell that she's hurting something awful."

Aaron peered through the spokes of the chair, which had now been stained on all sides. "What's she so *bedauerlich* about?"

Eli placed his hat back on his head with a grunt. "That's not my story to share, but she might share it with you… someday."

"Oh?"

"I was hoping that you could befriend her. Maybe you could offer to take her out to lunch or invite her to one of the gatherings for *die youngie*. She'll be living here for a couple of months, and she doesn't know anyone around these parts except for her *alt Daadi*. Having a close-in-age friend, someone to confide in, does wonders for the soul, *jah*?"

Aaron fidgeted with the paintbrush. Why, of all things, was Eli asking him to befriend Grace? Asking him to enter a social situation was like asking a fish to walk on land. How was he supposed to get to know Grace when he barely dared to look her in the eye? He struggled severely when it came to opening up to new people, and for that reason, he'd given up on ever finding love and starting a family of his own.

How can I turn Eli down after he's offered to give me his business? Aaron's hands trembled as he dipped the paintbrush back into the can of stain. Perhaps he'd been too hasty when he'd agreed to take over the woodshop.

"I guess I can try to talk with her sometime," he finally conceded as he began to stain the seat of the rocking chair, "though I can't promise that she'll be interested in talking with me. That's probably a lost cause."

Eli's face glowed with the warmth of a gas lantern. "All I ask is that you try, but I think you'll be pleasantly surprised by Gracie. She cares deeply for folks, and she's easy to talk to."

Aaron didn't look up from his work but nodded his response. *She'll have to be a very special woman to make any sort of connection with me.* Feeling prematurely defeated, he swiped the stain over the rocking chair's seat, wishing he hadn't felt so obligated to comply with Eli's request.

Chapter Two

The next morning was just as humid and hazy as the previous day had been, but Aaron enjoyed the brief buggy ride to work. A light fog lingered in the small valleys that were separated by rolling hills. Though the air was sticky, the scent of freshly cut and raked hay lingered like a spritz of expensive perfume. Like clockwork, a rooster's crow pierced the sleepy silence of each farm that the buggy passed by, and Aaron enjoyed his daily game of guessing which farm would host the loudest squawk that day.

When he arrived at Eli's property, he made quick work of unhitching his black horse, Clove. He made sure the gelding had a long drink of water before being released into the pasture where Eli's mare, Rosie, was already grazing on the dew-soaked grass.

As he left the barnyard and made his way toward the woodshop, he heard the squeaking of a door hinge that desperately needed to be oiled. He looked toward the cottage and saw Grace exiting the back door as she carried a basket of laundry. She scooted across the backyard to the two wooden poles that supported a clothesline that was rigged on a pulley system.

Aaron watched as Grace pulled several wooden clothespins out of her chore apron's pocket, then swiped one of

Eli's white Sunday shirts from the basket. She looked effortlessly graceful as she pinned the freshly washed laundry to the line. It was easy to see how well her name suited her.

Grace suddenly looked over her shoulder, as if she knew she was being watched. Aaron felt his chest tighten as their eyes met. He'd been caught staring and had potentially frightened the poor woman. Thoroughly embarrassed, Aaron dropped his gaze and started toward the woodshop, hoping that his awkwardness would quickly be forgotten.

"*Guder mariye*, Aaron!"

Aaron halted as a female voice called out to him. Was he hearing things? He hesitated and finally turned.

Grace wore a smile and raised her hand in a wave.

Startled by the friendly gesture, Aaron returned a small wave of his own.

When Grace gestured for him to come over to her, Aaron looked over his shoulder to see if Eli was approaching behind him. Surely Grace wasn't asking *him* to come over, not after the uncomfortable interaction they'd shared yesterday. But Eli wasn't behind him and nor was anyone else, so Aaron made his way over to Grace, his gaze darting between the cottage and the clothesline to keep from staring at her.

"My *daadi* told me the *gut* news," Grace said as Aaron approached, peeking around the shirt that she'd just hung on the clothesline. "You must be excited, *jah*?"

"W-what news?" Aaron asked as he came to a halt near the clothesline.

Grace bent and snatched another one of her grandfather's shirts out of the laundry basket. "He told me that you're running things in the woodshop and will be taking over permanently if everything works out."

"*Ach*, of course. I'm very *dankbaar* to be given such an opportunity," Aaron hastily replied. He felt his face grow warm and hoped that he'd conveyed his sincere gratitude to Eli's lovely granddaughter. "It came as a real shock."

"Really? Why's that?" Grace asked as she gave the shirt she was holding a good thrash, shaking out any wrinkles before they could set in. "My *daadi* must feel that you're more than capable of the job, or else he wouldn't have asked you to take over for him."

Aaron shifted his weight from one leg to the other. Grace probably knew nothing of his carpentry skills, other than what Eli had told her, but he still appreciated the compliment. He wanted to thank her for her encouragement, but the words just wouldn't seem to come out of his mouth.

A strained silence passed between them.

Aaron felt the need to break it. "I truly am *dankbaar* that Eli put so much faith in me, but I'm surprised he didn't want to keep the business in the *familye*."

Grace stuck some clothespins between her lips as she reached for a pair of black trousers. "The menfolk in our *familye* are dairymen," she said around pursed lips. She plucked the clothespins from her mouth and used them to pin the trousers to the line. "They've got herds to look after."

"*Jah*, Eli mentioned that most of your folks are farmers," Aaron responded as he watched Grace continue to hang the laundry. "It's a shame that you don't have a husband who's good with carpentry. If you did, the business could stay in the *familye*, even if it wasn't a blood relative who inherited it."

Grace was reaching to pin a bath towel to the line but suddenly froze in place. She shot Aaron a disapproving glare before she continued hanging the laundry. She quickly averted her gaze while the cordial countenance she'd previously shown disappeared from her face.

Aaron nervously fidgeted with the brim of his straw hat. Had he said something wrong? It certainly wouldn't be the first time in his life that he'd made a poor choice of words or found himself in an uneasy conversation due to his social clumsiness. Regardless of his good intentions, his extreme lack of self-confidence always seemed to play a part in ruining his conversations.

While Aaron was still deep in thought, worrying that he'd probably just upset his employer's granddaughter, Grace spoke up again.

"*Daadi* seems to be at peace about retiring, and we're all looking forward to spending more time with him once he moves into the new *daadi haus*." A lovely yet cautious grin crossed her face. "Instead of a long buggy ride or hiring a driver to visit him, I'll just have to take a few steps. That will be a *gut* change."

Aaron felt relieved that Grace was taking the reins of their conversation. "*Jah*, that will be nice. It must be a real pleasant surprise for your *familye*."

"You mean *Daadi*'s retiring and moving in with us?" Grace asked as she reached for several more clothespins. "It's no surprise. We've been offering to build a *daadi haus* onto our place for years now, but he only agreed to it recently. Besides, he's over eighty years *alt* and can't keep up with all that he used to. Mighty good time for someone to stop and smell the roses, *jah*?"

"*Jah*, but even though he's been slowing down he still

gets around so well," Aaron said as he inhaled the slightly soapy scent of the damp laundry. "I hope you won't get bored during your time here since Eli probably doesn't need you to do all that much."

Grace, who was now hidden behind a bedsheet that she'd just hung on the line, peered around the thin fabric, her accusing stare sharp enough to cut through some of the lumber in Eli's workshop. "Are you saying that my help isn't needed here?"

Aaron's heart jumped into his throat. He'd intended to compliment her grandfather for his strong will and perseverance, but Grace had clearly taken his comment as a personal insult.

"*Ach*, that's not what I meant at all," he said, retracting his statement. "Of course, your help is needed here. I just…what I meant to say was…"

"Excuse me," Grace interrupted as she bent to pick up the empty laundry basket. "I have a pie in the oven and I don't want it to burn." Without giving him a second glance, she marched past him and made her way back to the house.

That's just great, Aaron thought as he threw his head back and stared up at the overcast sky. *Every time I open my mouth, I stick my foot into it.*

How did Eli expect him to form a friendship with Grace when every time he spoke, he said the wrong thing? This had been his second strained interaction with her, and with his track record, it probably wouldn't be the last.

I doubt she's worried about a pie burning, Aaron grumbled to himself before he turned and plodded across the lawn toward the woodshop, where Eli was undoubtedly already working on one of their many projects.

* * *

Around fifty-thirty that evening, Grace hurried around Eli's little kitchen as she put the finishing touches on the bountiful dinner that she'd cooked. Excluding the light meals that she'd made since arriving yesterday morning, this was the first proper meal that Grace had cooked for her grandfather, and she put plenty of loving effort into preparing his favorite foods. She sliced into the juicy roasted chicken then set the serving platter in the middle of the small oak table before returning to the counter where she buttered the carrots, mashed potatoes, and noodles. The scent of a peach pie that she had baked earlier that afternoon lingered heavily in the kitchen as if to remind all who would partake of the meal to save room for dessert.

Grace grinned as she inhaled the aroma of the feast that she'd prepared and felt pleased with her work. She enjoyed preparing meals for loved ones and the looks on their faces when they tasted the fruits of her labor. Cooking each dish to perfection gave her nearly enough peace to forget about the bizarre interaction she'd had with Aaron King earlier that morning.

As she plated the dinner rolls that she'd baked after breakfast, she felt a frown creep back onto her face. Thoughts of Aaron's insulting statements moved to the front of her mind. Yesterday he'd been standoffish and today he'd not only reminded her of her singleness but also suggested that her help wasn't needed. Was he not paying attention to how his words could affect other people? Maybe he was simply a rude, ornery person.

The storm door suddenly squeaked open and Eli shuffled into the kitchen. He hung his tattered straw hat on one of the pegs near the door then inhaled deeply.

"*Ach du liva.* I can't remember the last time that this little kitchen smelled like a feast," he said as he moved to the sink and washed his hands. "Gracie, you went out of your way for your *alt Daadi.*"

Grace was pleased by her grandfather's genuine delight. "I hope you're *hungerich* because I made enough for us to have third and fourth helpings. Maybe we'll even have enough leftovers until the end of the week."

"*Gut* to hear, because I invited Aaron to stay for supper," Eli responded as he slowly made his way to the table.

As if on cue, the storm door creaked open again, and in came Aaron, his bowl-cut brown hair sticking to the perspiration on his forehead. He glanced around the room like a nervous puppy sniffing out an unfamiliar place. When his eyes landed on Grace, he immediately averted his gaze to the floor.

"*D-Denki* for inviting me to eat with you," he said as he hung his straw hat on an empty peg beside Eli's. "It smells real *gut.*"

"*Ach*, and it'll taste even better," Eli replied with a twinkle in his eyes. He motioned for Aaron to join him at the small, circular table.

With her back turned to them, Grace added a serving spoon to each side dish and resisted the urge to roll her eyes. She'd already had two awkward encounters with their young guest, and she wasn't looking forward to having a third. Knowing that she would be seeing the strange fellow every day while staying with *Daadi* here in Bird-in-Hand, Grace decided to take it in stride and treat Aaron with patience and kindness.

Once all the food was set out and Grace took her seat at the table, a silent prayer was said. When Eli lifted his head and cleared his throat, it signaled the end of the quiet moment of gratitude, and soon everyone was filling their plates with the mouth-watering dishes that Grace had prepared.

Eli forked a generous piece of chicken into his mouth and let out a pleasant sigh. "There's nothing better than a *gut* meal after a long day of work, ain't so?" He turned to Aaron and nodded ever so slightly.

Aaron looked up from his overflowing plate, his chocolate eyes landing first on Eli, then Grace. "Agreed. This is *appenditlich*, Grace."

"I'm glad you're enjoying it," Grace replied, though she wondered if Aaron truly liked her cooking or if he felt pressured by *Daadi* to compliment her.

There was no conversation for several minutes as everyone ate their meals. The only sound was that of silverware gently clinking against the dinner plates.

"So, how was your first full day in Bird-in-Hand, Gracie? Are you settling in well?" Eli asked as he dished a second helping of buttered noodles onto this plate.

"*Jah*," Grace replied as she looked up from her meal. "I don't think I've spent so much time in this *haus* since I was a little *maedel* and would beg *Mamm* and *Daed* to let me spend the weekend with you and *Mammi* Katie."

"*Ach*, what *gut* memories those are," Eli grinned. "And do you have everything you need?"

"I did a lot of laundry today and I noticed that some of your clothes need mending," Grace answered. "Would you happen to know where *Mammi*'s sewing supplies are?"

Eli let out a lighthearted scoff. "I gave the sewing kit to one of my *dochders* after *Mammi* went home to glory.

I thought it would be something nice and useful to re-member her by."

"That was very thoughtful of you," Grace commented before taking a sip of her water.

"There's a dry goods store, called Country Housewares that's only a few miles from here," Aaron suddenly chimed in, his voice squeaking on the last word of his sentence. When Grace and Eli turned their attention to him, he promptly turned beet red, as if embarrassed to have given input to the conversation.

"I could use a trip to the store," Grace said with a muted grin. "Is Country Housewares easy to find?"

Aaron nodded and used his fork to point to the right. "*Jah*, you just make a right out of here, then take another right when you get to Stumptown Road, and then…"

"Aaron, do you have any plans for tomorrow?" Eli inter-rupted. His glasses had slid down his nose and he peered over the lenses at their guest. "If you're not busy, maybe you can take Gracie to the store and show her around town a little, so she can familiarize herself with the area."

"*Ach*, that's not necessary." Grace was quick to protest. She was immediately uncomfortable when her grandfather put Aaron on the spot for her sake. Besides, she didn't want to spend any part of her Saturday with the aloof young man who probably wasn't interested in spending any time with her. "I'm sure Aaron would like to have a day to him-self without having to make the trip over here. Maybe you and I can go to Country Housewares tomorrow, and we can shop for anything you need as well."

Eli shook his head as he cut one of the dinner rolls into halves. "Everything I need is already in this *haus*, and my arthritis is acting up too much to climb into and out of the buggy."

Grace was almost certain that she'd seen her grandfather wink subtly at Aaron before slathering a huge glob of butter onto his bread.

Aaron, who'd been leaning over his plate, suddenly straightened in his seat. "I've got nothing better to do tomorrow." He paused. "What I mean is, I can certainly take you to the store and point out other places that might be of interest to you while you're in Bird-in-Hand."

"*Denki*." Grace voiced her gratitude through gritted teeth.

"*Gaern gschehne*. Should I pick you up around ten o'clock?"

"*Jah*, that would be *oll recht*," she answered softly, unable to muster any enthusiasm.

She noticed Eli's glass of iced tea was near empty so she stood and made her way to the refrigerator to get the pitcher. She opened the heavy door and leaned into the chilled container, taking a moment to groan inwardly. Unable to control her expression any longer, she allowed her lips to droop into a frown and rolled her eyes. She was dreading tomorrow's outing with Aaron. From his unenthused offer of assistance to his tense grin, it was plain to see that he was equally thrilled about tomorrow's plans.

Grace rearranged a few of the things in the refrigerator, using the time to settle her nerves and push down her frustrations. She took a deep breath and reminded herself that everyone, no matter how strange or introverted, deserved kindness.

She removed the pitcher from the refrigerator and closed

the door. As she padded back to the table, she sent up a quick prayer for patience. Hopefully, the Saturday outing with Aaron King would go smoothly and also would be a one-time occurrence.

Chapter Three

When Aaron arrived home that evening, he made quick work of unhitching his horse. The dinner he'd shared with Eli and Grace Ebersol had been downright tasty, but also exhausting. Socializing, if you could call it that, with Grace had been as awkward as juggling cats, causing his self-doubt to stalk him like a hungry tiger. Try as he might, he couldn't rouse the confidence needed to have a decent conversation with a stranger, especially when that stranger was as lovely as Grace.

"And now I have to take her to the store tomorrow," Aaron muttered to Clove as he led the jet-black horse toward the barn. "I'll probably say or do something *schtupid* and embarrass myself."

With every ounce of his being, he wished he hadn't agreed to take Grace on the errand, but how could he have said no? For one thing, Eli had put him on the spot by asking the favor in front of Grace. Secondly, there was the promise he'd made to Eli to try to warm up to his lovely granddaughter. How would he ever win her over without spending time with her? For a second time in as many days, Aaron found himself unable to say no to his employer.

Aaron grumbled inwardly, scolding himself for lacking

the tenacity that every other young man seemed to have. He fretted over his shortcomings and tomorrow's plans with Grace as he led Clove to one of the empty horse stalls.

As he rubbed down the gelding and made sure that he had plenty of water, Aaron heard the small, gentle voice of a young girl. His apprehension immediately vanished when he realized his nine-year-old sister, Annie, was nearby. For whatever reason, Annie looked up to him as if he was her hero, and the two shared a very special bond. Out of his six brothers and sisters, he could always count on talkative, cheerful Annie to brighten his day.

Aaron followed the sound of Annie's voice to one of the empty horse stalls. He found his young sibling nestled comfortably in the fresh bedding with a gray mother cat and her litter of five kittens. Since the day the little critters had been born, Annie spent nearly every waking moment watching and holding the little balls of fur.

"I thought I'd find you here with the *katz*," Aaron said as he leaned against the stall's door and gazed down at the sweet scene before him.

Annie, who was petting the smallest kitten, looked up and gave her brother a winning smile. "*Kumme* and play with the *busslin* with me."

Aaron grinned as he entered the horse stall, plopped down beside his sister, and picked up a black-and-white kitten as it toddled toward him. "Are you babysitting these *busslin* again?"

"*Jah*, someone has to watch them," Annie replied, cuddling the little orange kitten close to her heart.

"What about the mama cat?" Aaron asked, amused by his sister's innocent antics.

"She's sleeping, so I'm keeping an eye on her babies

until she wakes up." Annie gestured to the fluffy gray mother cat, whose whiskers and paws were twitching in slumber. "I'm glad that you're home. I was gonna ask you to give me a ride to Rachel Lapp's *haus* tomorrow. I told her that she could have one of the *busslin*, and I think she'd like this orange one."

"It's nice of you to offer one of the *busslin* to your *freind*, but the *busslin* still need to be with their *mamm* for a few more weeks. Once they're a little older, I'll be glad to give you and the chosen *bussli* a ride to Rachel's *haus*."

Annie nodded, accepting his answer. "Can we go fishing tomorrow instead? And maybe afterward we can get some ice cream cones?"

Aaron thought a relaxing day spent fishing on the bank of Mill Creek followed by an ice cream treat sounded wonderful, and he nearly agreed to the plan before his commitment to Grace rushed to the front of his mind.

"*Ach*, I'm sorry, Annie. I've made plans for tomorrow," he said regretfully as the kitten he held snuggled close to his chest. "How about we go fishing next Saturday?"

Annie put the orange kitten next to its mother, then picked up the largest one, which was plump and all white, resembling a little marshmallow. "You never have anything planned on Saturdays," she said as her large brown eyes questioned him. "What are you gonna be doing?"

"You know Eli Ebersol, the man I work for?"

Annie nodded.

"His *enkelin* will be visiting for the next few weeks, and she doesn't know her way around Bird-in-Hand all that well." He paused, feeling his heart rate increase at even the thought of spending time with Grace. "I'm taking her to Country Housewares tomorrow so she can do some shopping."

Annie's eyebrows furrowed as she continued to stroke the white kitten. "Why isn't her *daadi* taking her?"

I've wondered the very same thing, Aaron scoffed to himself. He did not doubt that Eli was in pain due to his arthritis, but still, the old fellow seemed tickled by the opportunity to match him and Grace up for the errand. Could it be that Eli was trying to give him a helpful nudge in his quest to win Grace over?

"Aaron?"

"Eli's not getting around as well as he used to," Aaron answered, hoping that his kid sister wouldn't notice the hesitance in his voice. He fought to put on a happy face for her sake.

"*Jah*, I noticed he's been acting kinda shaky and tired at church lately." She reached over and patted his hand. "It's awful nice of you to help his *enkelin* get her shopping done. That's what *Gott* would want you to do."

Aaron stared down at the black-and-white kitten that had fallen asleep against his chest. He soaked up Annie's encouragement, though he was certain that she didn't know just how badly he needed it. But, of course, Annie had no idea that he hadn't been the one to offer his help, and that he was dreading every moment of the outing with Grace Ebersol.

"Is this lady your *aldi*, Aaron?"

His sister's question startled Aaron so thoroughly that he flinched, waking up the sleeping kitten. The little feline squirmed wildly until he placed it against the mother cat.

"*Nee*, she's not my *aldi*. She's just a *freind*," Aaron quickly responded. He suddenly felt too warm and wanted to escape the muggy barn. "W-what would make you think that she and I are courting?"

Annie shrugged, lifted the white kitten, and rubbed its fuzzy fur against her cheek. "*Vell*, you never spend time with any ladies, other than those in our *familye*. Ain't so?"

Aaron guffawed at Annie's pointed yet innocent remark. "I guess I can't argue with that." Truthfully, he couldn't let his thoughts linger on his sister's statement without falling into a pit of melancholy that he might never have the strength to crawl out of. He longed to fall in love with a special woman and start a family of his own, but until he believed in himself enough to pursue a godly woman, that dream would never come to fruition.

"Can I go to the store with you and that lady tomorrow?" Annie asked, looking as hopeful as a springtime sunrise. "I've got six dollars in change saved up, and I'd sure like to look at the book section."

Aaron's first reaction was to tell Annie that he would take her to the store another time, fearing that Grace might be put out by an unexpected third party on their outing. But on second thought, having talkative Annie around would certainly take the pressure off of him to make conversation. Plus, being in the presence of someone he knew well might counteract the apprehension he felt around his new acquaintance.

"*Jah*, of course, you can come along," Aaron said to his sister as he playfully tapped the tip of her button nose. "Maybe you can show Grace around the store since you're the best shopper that I know."

Annie giggled, and her laughter warmed Aaron's heart. Then the girl changed the topic of their conversation to the tomatoes that she'd helped their mother can that morning.

Aaron listened to what his sister had to say, but he wasn't able to move past the image of a tense-looking Grace that remained cemented in his mind. Grace's turquoise eyes had nearly bugged out of her head when her grandfather had suggested that they ride to the store together. Clearly, she shared his feelings of dread regarding tomorrow's unexpected arrangement.

Oh well, Aaron said to himself. *Hopefully, Annie and Grace will do most of the talking. Lord knows that if the conversation is left up to me, I'll just make a fool of myself.*

At sunset, Grace and her grandfather sat on the cottage's back porch that overlooked a neighboring farm's grazing pasture. Half of the twenty-or-so Jersey cattle that occupied the space grazed peacefully, while the other half laid down, chewing their cud and lowing contentedly to each other. Crickets chirped and lightning bugs sparkled their way through Eli's tidy backyard, some clustering around the hydrangea bush that was heavy with blue blossoms.

Sitting in a rocking chair adjacent to her grandfather, Grace held a cross-stitching project that she'd been working on for the past few weeks. She suddenly realized that she hadn't sewn a single stitch that evening, having been unable to focus on her favorite hobby. She glanced down at the off-white aida cloth and gently ran her fingertips over the dozens of tiny stitches she'd sewn in the shapes of various wildflowers, wishing that she felt as bright and cheerful as the scene she'd created.

"Penny for your thoughts, Gracie."

"*Ach*, I'm not thinking about anything in particular."

She mustered a smile for her grandfather's sake. "Would you like me to bring you another slice of peach pie?"

Eli shook his head. "I couldn't eat another bite." He gave his stomach a few slow thumps. "I haven't eaten myself this full since last Christmas supper. It's *wunderbaar gut* to have such a nice meal for no special reason. Reminds me of when your *Mammi* Katie was alive, and I'd eat like a king every day."

Grace grinned, though the memory of her late grandmother was bittersweet. "I'm *hallich* to fix any meals or desserts you like. Is there anything special you'd like to have tomorrow?"

Eli folded his calloused hands and placed them in his lap. "What I'd like is to know why you've been so quiet since supper."

Grace was amused by her grandfather's persistence. Still, she didn't want to burden him with her troubles. "I guess I've just got a lot on my mind tonight."

"You just said that you weren't thinking about anything."

She let out a playful scoff. *Daadi* might be getting up in years, but his mind was still as sharp as a tack. "Truthfully, I was thinking about that errand that I'll be running tomorrow." She felt her face warm and hoped that *Daadi* wouldn't see her blush. "I don't want to be disrespectful, but it would be a lie if I said that I was pleased about spending time with Aaron."

Eli nodded and worked his mouth, his gray beard bouncing with each slight movement. "Why's that, Gracie?"

Grace purposefully bit her tongue, buying herself some time to carefully choose her words. "I feel a little awkward about taking up a portion of Aaron's Saturday. After all, we barely know each other."

Eli said nothing, as if knowing that wasn't the full story.

"He...he also seems uncomfortable around me," Grace added hesitantly, as she drummed her fingers on the armrest of the rocking chair. "He's just so quiet, and when he does speak up, he says the strangest things."

Eli's gray, overgrown eyebrows rose as he chuckled. "You've got a point there. Aaron is the quiet type, for sure and for certain, but I've never met a kinder man." He coughed several times then cleared his throat. "Sounds to me like you might have things *verhuddelt*."

"What do you mean?"

"*Vell*, you said that Aaron is uncomfortable around you, but maybe you're uncomfortable around him."

Grace stifled a laugh and shook her head. "And just how do you know that?"

"I'm your *Daadi*," he grinned, his eyes twinkling with a great fondness for her. "I've known you since you first came into this world. I've watched you grow from a pink-faced *boppli* into a lovely *yung* woman. Twenty-three years is plenty of time to get to know a person, *jah*?"

"*Jah*, I suppose so," Grace conceded, enjoying the sweet moment with her favorite relative.

"I don't want you to isolate yourself," Eli went on. "Aaron just wants to be your *freind*, and not one person on *Gott*'s earth is in any position to turn down friendship."

Grace understood her grandfather's sentiment, but the last thing she wanted to do was allow herself to become vulnerable, especially to a man. Her lingering pain from being blindsided by her longtime former beau still felt raw. Even the possibility of having a new friend seemed too risky. Truth be told, she would prefer to keep to herself during most of her waking hours.

"I don't know," Grace finally admitted. "Friendships that are meant to be usually just happen on their own, *jah*?"

"But wouldn't our Heavenly Father want us to be *freind* with everyone?"

"You're right, as usual," Grace replied, appreciating her grandfather's wisdom, even if the notion of becoming friendly with Aaron King felt as prickly as walking barefoot through a meadow full of thistles.

"Who knows," Eli continued as he watched a small, brown rabbit hop out of the hydrangea bush to nibble on some nearby clover. "If you and Aaron enjoy each other's company, you might even end up going to one of the events for *die youngie*."

"*Nee*, I won't do that." Grace's objection came firm and swift, like a sudden strike of lightning on a humid summer night.

"Why not? Would that be such a bad thing?" Eli asked as he turned his attention from the rabbit to his granddaughter.

Unable to voice her deep heartache, she decided not to verbalize her objections. Instead, she lowered her head and stared down at the cross-stitch project that rested in her lap, the brightly colored stitches in the cloth almost mocking the gloom that she felt.

"I understand how you feel, Gracie. When we've been hurt, our first instinct is to not allow the hurt to happen again," Eli said gently. "But as followers of *Gott*, we have to choose to give Him our pain rather than to hang onto it."

Grace said nothing to that.

"The desire to isolate yourself is a result of hanging onto your pain." Eli gave a cautious grin and then slowly stood with a grunt. "I think it's about time for me to turn in. *Gut nacht*, Gracie."

"*Gut nacht*," Grace whispered as her grandfather shuffled past her and entered the house. She remained seated on the rocking chair, feeling her eyes fill with tears as she considered her grandfather's words. Certainly, he hadn't intended to upset her, but any amount of time Grace spent remembering how she'd been jilted caused her to well up.

Blinking rapidly and allowing her tears to spill down her cheeks, Grace sat silently, sniffling now and then as nightfall settled in and stars began to sparkle. Though the evening was as peaceful as a mother's soothing lullaby, Grace felt little peace in her soul.

I won't put my heart on the line again, Grace thought as she slowly inhaled the cool night air, trying her best to settle her emotions. *I won't open up, no matter how many others think I should, especially not to Aaron King.*

Chapter Four

"Gracie, a buggy just pulled in. Looks like Aaron's here to pick you up."

"Be right there," Grace called to her grandfather as she stood in her temporary bedroom. She looked down at her mint green dress and black cape apron to make sure that it was free of stains or wrinkles. Then she glanced in the small, square mirror that hung on the wall, making sure that her hair was neatly parted in the middle, and no strands had come loose from the low bun that she had styled earlier. She placed her organdy, heart-shaped *kapp* over her hair, pinned the head-covering in place, then took one final peek at her reflection.

Goodness, what's come over me? Grace clicked her tongue at herself. She had never been the type to primp and fuss over her appearance, as it was frowned upon in her Plain community. She was neat and tidy, and that's what mattered. Besides, it wasn't like she needed to impress anyone, including Aaron King.

Allowing herself to release a heavy sigh, she grabbed her brown leather purse from its spot on her dresser, then marched out of the room.

When she reached the quiet sitting room, she found her grandfather seated on the sofa with the most recent edition of *The Budget* newspaper in hand. She noticed that the pages of the newspaper were vibrating ever so slightly, and she wondered if it was caused by the frequent breeze from the nearby open window or her grandfather's unsteady hands.

"Is there anything you want from the store?" Grace asked, peeking her face into the room.

Eli lowered his paper to get a better look at her. "*Jah*, I want you to have a *gut* time."

Grace couldn't help but grin at her grandfather's comment, even though today's outing wouldn't bring her any amount of joy.

"I fixed you a turkey sandwich and made a fresh pitcher of meadow tea in case we aren't back in time for the noon meal," Grace said over her shoulder as she entered the kitchen and headed for the door, though she hoped to return home sooner rather than later. "If you're still hungry, there's leftover…"

"*Ach*, I'll be just fine," Eli interrupted her. "Don't worry about me, and take your time shopping. Maybe Aaron will even want to treat you to lunch while you're out."

Grace doubted that would happen and even hoped that it wouldn't, but didn't voice that opinion. Instead, she simply smiled and said a quick farewell before hurrying outside.

As she made her way across the lawn, Grace saw Aaron sitting on the driver's side of the buggy. He was speaking softly, though she was unable to make out what he said. Had she caught him talking to himself?

When she called out a greeting that sounded much more cheerful than she felt, Aaron finally glanced in her direction. He took one of his hands off the reins and raised it in a half-hearted wave.

Looks like he's thrilled to be going out with me, Grace noticed. Why, if she wasn't so perturbed, she might find their mutual lack of enthusiasm to be humorous.

Seconds later, an Amish girl who was sitting in the buggy's back seat peeked out of the rig, smiling shyly and staring curiously. The girl, who was probably younger than ten years old, had hair much darker than Aaron's. However, her warm, brown eyes were nearly identical to his, making it very clear that they were related.

"*Guder mariye,*" Grace said as she stepped up to the buggy, focusing her attention more on the adorable child than Aaron.

"Hello," the girl beamed at her. "My name is Annie King."

"This is my little *schweschder,*" Aaron added, sounding a little more chipper than he usually did. "When she heard that I was going to Country Housewares, she wanted to come along. I hope that's *oll recht.*"

"Of course it is," Grace replied and she climbed into the left side of the buggy and took a seat beside Aaron. She looked over her shoulder and grinned at the young girl. "I'm Grace Ebersol. It's *gut* to meet you, Annie."

Annie returned a smile that was nearly as bright as the sun. She fiddled with the edge of her black cape apron that was nearly identical to the one that Grace wore. "I'm glad you came out of the *haus* right away, 'cause I'm excited to get to the store."

Aaron chuckled and clicked his tongue to get his horse moving. "She's been talking about going shopping all morning." He glanced over his shoulder and gave his sister a wink. "Let's get going so you don't jump out of the buggy and run all the way there."

When Annie giggled sweetly, Grace felt a sudden wave of relief. She'd been expecting itchy silence and bumbling conversation, but Annie's presence seemed to put Aaron at ease, which made Grace more comfortable as well. Perhaps she'd unfairly judged him after their two earlier interactions. True, he was somewhat awkward, but maybe he was just shy around folks that he didn't know well.

One thing is for certain, today is going to be better than I expected, Grace thought as she settled against the rig's bench seat.

Aaron guided the horse onto the quiet country lane, and they were off. The gelding clip-clopped down the road, pulling the buggy past pastures of grazing cattle and fields of corn, wheat, and soybeans. The crops swayed ever so slightly in the warm breeze, and the patchwork of natural colors reminded Grace of an old quilt airing on a clothesline.

As they headed away from Bird-in-Hand and made their way toward the neighboring village of Leola, Aaron pointed out homes and farms where members of their church district lived, as well as a Mennonite-run bulk foods store, a harness shop, and a fabric store.

It wasn't long before Annie chimed in, leaning between Aaron and Grace from her spot in the back seat. "I had six dollars, but Aaron gave me another five before we left our *haus* today. I bet I'll have enough to buy two new books."

Grace grinned at Annie's eagerness. The child reminded her of herself when she was younger. "That was nice of your *bruder.*"

Aaron briefly took his eyes off the road to glance at Grace. A hint of a blush crept up his neck and spread to his cheeks.

"*Jah*, it is. Aaron is the best big *bruder* ever," Annie went on, now leaning against the front seat, so much so that Grace wondered if she would climb over the bench and squeeze into the spot between her and Aaron. "He always does fun things with me."

Grace's heart warmed at Annie's obvious affection for her brother. It reminded her of the close bond that she shared with her siblings.

"What kinds of things do you do together?" she asked, surprised to learn that Aaron wasn't always the stiff, brooding type.

"*Ach*, lots of stuff. We play catch and board games. Sometimes we take my pony, Bonnie, out for a cart ride, and I almost always drive," Annie said, her face aglow with excitement. "We go fishing too, but Aaron likes that more than I do." She scrunched up her cute little button nose. "I don't like baiting the hooks with slimy worms, but Aaron doesn't mind."

Grace chuckled and turned her attention to Aaron. "Is that so?"

Aaron, realizing that the attention had fallen on him, looked startled. He glanced at Grace, tensed up, and then returned his eyes to the road. "*Jah*, I suppose you could say that's true." His mouth twisted into a little smirk like he was hesitant to let out a laugh. "It's not polite to do all the talking, so maybe we should ask Grace something about herself."

Annie comically tapped her chin and furrowed her brow. "Let me think of a *gut* question."

Grace and Aaron exchanged amused looks, and for the first time since meeting him, she felt nearly at ease in his presence. If things kept going so well between them, maybe they really could become friends.

"Do you have *brieder* or *schweschdre*?" Annie asked, interrupting Grace's realization.

Grace bobbed her head. "I am the youngest of six *kinner*. I have two *brieder* and three *schweschdre*. I'm closest to Abby, probably because she is only two years older than me."

Annie's eyes widened. "You're just like me! I'm also the youngest, but our family has five *kinner*, and I'm the only *maedel*." Her smile dimmed. "You must miss your home and your *familye*, ain't so?"

"I do," Grace admitted wistfully. "But I have my *Daadi* here, and I'm sure I'll make new *freind* too."

Annie's infectious grin returned. "Aaron and I will be your *freind* and that will help you feel more at home while you're here. Right, Aaron?"

"Of course," Aaron replied. He gave a timid smile. "If there's anything you ever need, Grace, you can count on us."

"*Denki*. I appreciate that very much." Grace turned and focused on the cluster of weeping willow trees they were passing. She was deeply moved by the sincere offer of friendship from Aaron and his sister, and she felt somewhat guilty for judging this young fellow so harshly upon their first meeting.

"We can always use more *freind*, *jah*?" Annie's sweet voice interrupted Grace's soul-searching. "Aaron doesn't have that many *freind*, especially lady *freind*, since he's so shy."

Annie's innocent yet blunt remark seemed to strike a chord in Aaron. He pinched his eyes shut for a moment.

The hint of a blush that he'd worn earlier intensified, and suddenly he was beet red.

"Our oldest *bruder*, Noah, is the least shy person in the whole world," Annie said, blissfully unaware of the obvious embarrassment she'd just inflicted on her brother. "He can walk up to a stranger and become *freind* right away. Ain't that so, Aaron?"

"*Vell*, we can't all be perfect like Noah." His lips curled into an awkward grin. "So, G-Grace," he stumbled over his words, "is there anywhere else you'd like to go while we're out?"

Grace thanked him for the offer, then said that she might be interested in stopping at the fabric store that they'd passed earlier if it wouldn't be any trouble.

Aaron assured her that it was no bother at all.

Before he had a chance to say anything else, Annie started chattering again, pointing to the one-room schoolhouse that she attended as the small building came into view.

Grace listened as Annie talked about the games that she and her friends played during recess, but she found herself unable to focus her attention on the child's stories. Instead, she stole glances at Aaron, hoping her curiosity would remain unnoticed. It was clear to see that there was...something hiding behind his eyes. Frustration? Defeat? Sadness?

Grace pitied the strange fellow who sat beside her. There was a lot more to him than what she'd first noticed. Though the notion of becoming friends with Aaron seemed as unlikely as a blizzard in July, she couldn't deny a small yet steady magnetic pull toward him.

I'll remember him in my prayers, and I'll do my best

to be an encouraging friend, Grace decided, hoping that whatever was ailing Aaron could be mended with a little kindness and support.

Aaron held back as the trio entered Country Housewares, unsure of what to do. The familiar store that catered to the Plain community, lit by natural sunlight and gas lamps, was as welcoming as usual, but he felt slightly out of place. He wasn't shopping for anything in particular, and he wasn't one to browse for fun.

His initial plan was to simply tag along with Grace and Annie, but that changed when Annie immediately took off toward the book aisle. He'd expected his sister to stick close to Grace since the child seemed enamored with her, but he hadn't considered her love for children's chapter books.

What should I do now? Aaron wondered as he watched Grace take a shopping cart and start down the first aisle, which contained some tools and gardening supplies on one side and cooking utensils on the other. He could go after Annie, which was certainly the more comfortable choice, but he didn't feel right about leaving Grace to wander the unfamiliar store on her own.

Deciding to go after Eli's granddaughter, Aaron headed for the aisle that she'd gone down. He spotted her looking at a bird feeder that was in the shape of a sunflower, then examining the price tag that was attached to it.

She must've heard the squeak of his boots on the spotless, shining floor. Looking over at him, she offered a friendly, closed-mouthed smile.

Aaron wanted to say something witty, or maybe simply offer his assistance. He opened his mouth to speak, but before any words came out Grace had pushed her still-empty cart down the aisle to resume her shopping.

He puffed out a deep breath as quietly as he could. If only he had the confidence to walk up to her and start a conversation! He moved to the spot where Grace had been standing and pretended to look at the selection of bird feeders and birdseed before inching down the aisle again. He halted a few steps away from her as she stopped to inspect some cookware. When Grace picked up a muffin tin, he moved forward again but froze when she looked his way.

"Are you following me?" she asked in a playful tone, raising one of her eyebrows.

Aaron's chest tensed up and he reached to rub the back of his neck. "*Jah.*"

Grace's mouth fell open ever so slightly and she stared at him in bewilderment.

"I mean… I am following you, but I wanted to offer my help with finding the things you are shopping for." He forced himself to look at the various pots, pans, tins, and bowls. He found himself unable to maintain eye contact with Grace for longer than a few seconds. It was almost as if her piercing blue eyes could see right into his soul, and that was something he'd never experienced before. If he was being honest with himself, the feeling wasn't at all unpleasant.

"*Denki,*" Grace said as she placed the muffin tin in her cart and then pulled a slip of paper out of her purse. "The next thing on my list is a spool of black thread or a small sewing kit that contains thread."

"I think that would be a few aisles over," Aaron said with a shrug. "I've never shopped for anything related to sewing, so I could be wrong." He scoffed at himself. "Some help I am, huh?"

Grace started forward, pushing the shopping cart once again. "Let's go find out if you are right or if you are no help." She gave him a playful wink, then headed around the corner and disappeared into the next aisle.

Aaron chuckled, feeling more at ease around his new friend. He could see that Grace was kindhearted and had a good sense of humor. She selflessly came to her grandfather's aid, so she clearly cared for the wellbeing of others. She was also an excellent cook and a true natural beauty. A real catch, Aaron noted.

As he followed Grace up the neighboring aisle, he found himself wondering why she didn't have a beau. Surely, any young man would be eager to win her affection. *Including me, if I had anything to offer her*, he thought glumly as familiar self-doubt clung to him like the sticky filling of a shoofly pie.

Grace suddenly gasped loudly, rattling Aaron out of his thoughts. "*Wass iss letz*?" he asked, hurrying forward to catch up with her.

"*Ach*, nothing's wrong. I just spotted some blackberry jam." She pointed toward the small selection of locally made jams and jellies. "I used to pick blackberries every summer and bring them to my *Mammi*. She would make enough jars of jam to last me until the following summer since that was my favorite flavor." The upward curve of her lips fell slightly. "I haven't had blackberry jam since she passed away," she said, her voice suddenly softer.

Aaron's heart went out to Grace. He counted himself blessed that all of his grandparents, and even his great-grandparents, were still alive. He couldn't imagine the pain of losing a beloved family member, or anyone that he loved for that matter.

He gave Grace a reassuring grin then snatched a jar of the special jam off the shelf.

"Is blackberry your favorite flavor too?" Grace asked, brightening up and seemingly recovered from her brief, bittersweet journey down memory lane.

"*Nee*, I've never cared for the taste of blackberry," he said as he studied the pretty label on the jar. "I'm partial to peach and apricot."

Grace took another look at the display, then gestured to the jams and jellies. "Then why not get the peach jam?"

Aaron shook his head. "I'm not shopping for jam."

Grace stared at him blankly, glanced down at the jar in his hand, then locked eyes with him once more.

"I'm getting this jam for you," he explained.

"*Ach*, that's awful nice of you, but you don't have to do that," she said as she held her hand out to him. "I can certainly pay for my own jam," she continued, her voice catching on a giggle.

"*Nee*, I'd like to get it for you as a *denki* for that *appenditlich* supper that you made," Aaron insisted as he held the jar high above his head, far away from Grace's reach.

"*Vell* then, I'll just have to make sure I cook big suppers often, *jah*?"

Aaron couldn't stop himself from chuckling at that remark.

The pair continued with their browsing, slowly making their way up and down the aisles of the store as Grace crossed items off her shopping list, including the thread, which was right where Aaron had imagined it would be. They shopped without saying much to each other, yet

Aaron found the amiable silence between them to be strangely comfortable.

As they strolled down an aisle that displayed stunning sets of fine china, Grace stopped in her tracks and frowned.

"Is everything *oll recht*?" Aaron ventured, nervously hoping that Grace hadn't found the silence between them to be unpleasant.

Grace ran her fingertips around the golden rim of a shiny white soup bowl. "I have a set of brand-new china in my hope chest that looks just like this. I've been looking to get rid of it for a while. Do you think this store would buy them from me on consignment?"

"I don't think so, but it wouldn't hurt to ask an employee," Aaron replied, baffled by Grace's sudden change in disposition. "Do you have two sets of dishes?"

"*Nee*, why do you ask?"

"I was just thinking that it's kind of strange for a *maedel* of marriage age to be looking to sell items from her hope chest."

Grace narrowed her eyes but said nothing.

"I mean…w-won't you need a set of dishes when you marry and start a *familye* of your own? Why sell them?" Aaron asked, stumbling over his words. The way that Grace stared him down caused his palms to start sweating, and he tightened his grip on the jar of jam, lest it fall and smash to pieces.

Grace's slender shoulders slumped as she gave the beautiful tableware one last look. "To be frank, Aaron, I don't think that's any of your business."

Aaron cringed at her reaction and realized that he'd unknowingly brought up a sore topic. Things had been going so well between them, and just as usual, he'd gone and said the wrong thing.

"I'm sorry, I didn't mean to…"

"That's *oll recht*," Grace interrupted him, though the glum downward curve of her lips let Aaron know that things were far from all right. "Let's just get this shopping done." She pushed the shopping cart forward without waiting for Aaron to respond.

Just when things were starting to go well, he said the wrong thing. Eli had made a mistake in asking him to befriend Grace, he thought to himself. *I can always be counted on to mess things up.*

Chapter Five

❧

"Last one to the buggy is a rotten *oi*," Annie shouted as the trio exited the store. She took off running down the sidewalk, rounded the corner of the building, and was promptly out of sight.

Grace didn't feel like running, but she did feel like a rotten egg. She peeked over her shoulder at Aaron as he followed her down the sidewalk. He'd insisted on carrying her shopping bags, though they weren't overly heavy.

She shouldn't have spoken to him so harshly, and regret seeped into her like water leaking into a damaged boat. Aaron couldn't have possibly known that she'd been jilted by her longtime sweetheart. Since she would never allow herself to fall in love for a second time and risk such heartache again, the idea of marriage was totally out of the question. Yet Aaron's innocent remark about selling her hope chest items tore open a wound that never seemed to fully heal.

She listened to the gentle tinkling of the wind chimes that hung from the store's eaves as she and Aaron continued along the sidewalk, though the peaceful, metallic melody didn't soothe her. Once memories of her former beau floated to the front of her mind, it felt impossible to

think of anything else besides the intense grief and loneliness that the breakup had caused her.

"Did you find everything you were looking for?" Aaron
quietly asked, breaking into her internal stream of self-
pity.

"I did. *Denki* for bringing me," Grace answered as she
forced a weak smile, "and for carrying my bags."

"*Gaern gschehne.*" He looked away from her, focusing
his gaze on the sea of green cornstalks across the street
from the store. "Should we head to the fabric store next?"

"I'm all worn out. Would it be *oll recht* if we just went
home?" Grace had planned to purchase a few yards of ma-
terial to make her grandfather a new pair of trousers and
a dress for herself. But after the reminders of her failed
relationship and the fact that her chance at finding love
had been pummeled into the dust, the idea of shopping no
longer appealed. She longed to simply return to the cottage and hide in the solitude of her temporary bedroom,
though she could never hide from the sharp dagger of disappointment that never seemed to dull.

"*Jah*, that's fine with me," Aaron said solemnly. "Grace,
I'm sorry if I—"

"*Ach*, Aaron! Didn't think I'd be seeing you today."

Aaron's apology was interrupted by an elderly Amish
woman who rounded the corner and shuffled toward them.
Her hair was as white as freshly fallen snow and her wrinkles were as deep as the Susquehanna River. She was a
tiny thing, though her hunched-over posture made her
seem even smaller.

"Hello, *Aendi*," Aaron greeted the woman, speaking
loudly and slowly. "This is my great-*aendi*, Sarah King,"
he said, gesturing to his great-aunt. "This is Grace Eb-

ersol," he continued, still speaking at a higher volume than usual. "She's Eli Ebersol's *kinnskind*, visiting from Paradise."

As he introduced her, Aaron gently rested his hand on Grace's shoulder. Grace jumped ever so slightly, startled by the abrupt fluttering of butterflies in her stomach. Surely that had only been caused by the surprise of Aaron's gentle touch.

"It's *gut* to meet you," Grace greeted the little old woman.

Sarah stepped closer and turned her left ear toward them. "What's that?"

"I said it's *gut* to meet you," Grace said a bit more loudly as she took one of Sarah's gnarled hands and gave it a few quick squeezes.

"*Ach*, it's *gut* to meet you too, dear." She glanced up at her nephew and wiggled her white eyebrows playfully. "*Wunderbaar gut*, indeed!"

Aaron quickly removed his hand from Grace's shoulder as he shot her a sheepish glance.

"How long will you be staying in Bird-in-Hand, Grace?" Sarah asked.

Grace explained that she was staying with her grandfather for the time being, until he was ready to move into the new *daadi haus* on her father's farm.

"*Vell* then, I'll look forward to seeing you at our church meetings." Sarah blinked up at Grace, her brown eyes largely magnified through the thick lenses of her glasses. "Word has it that there's gonna be a Sisters' Day gathering within the next month or so, and you're more than *wilkumme* to join us."

"*Denki* for the invitation." Grace smiled down at Sarah,

feeling like she'd known the grandmotherly woman for years. "I'll look forward to it."

"*Gut*, so will I. Now I best get my shopping done so I can get home in time for dinner." Sarah pointed a bony finger at the empty tote bag that hung on the crook of her arm. "It may still be an hour before the noon meal, but I'm no longer a spring chicken and things take me longer than they used to. *Mache gute*." With that, she continued shuffling toward the store's entrance.

"Did you need any help, *aendi*?" Aaron called after her. "Why don't I follow you home and help you carry your things inside?"

Sarah stopped and turned halfway around. "I may move slowly, but I can manage on my own, Aaron. You take care of your lovely *yung* lady," she replied, pointing at Grace. "Such a handsome couple."

Before Aaron or Grace could say anything, Sarah opened the shop's door and disappeared inside.

Aaron and Grace exchanged stunned glances.

"S-sorry about that," Aaron sputtered.

"No need to be sorry," Grace replied, still holding back a chuckle. "She's absolutely charming."

"*Jah*, but I should have explained that we aren't a couple." He took off his straw hat and fanned his face for a few seconds before placing the hat back on his head. "For someone who claims to move slowly, she certainly hustled into the store. I didn't even have a second to respond." He chewed on his lower lip. "That was almost as awkward as I am."

Grace let loose with the laughter that she could no longer hold back. Much to her surprise, Aaron joined in, and soon they were both nearly doubled over in a fit of giggles.

"That was a *gut* one," Grace said after finally catching her breath, "but sometimes I think you're awful hard on yourself."

Aaron shrugged as they rounded the corner of the shop and made their way toward the hitching rail, where his horse patiently waited, his long ebony tail flicking away the occasional fly. "You're probably right," he admitted, "but I don't know any other way to be."

That comment tugged on Grace's heartstrings. As they walked toward the buggy, she almost reached over to hold his hand but quickly nixed the idea. She wouldn't want the gesture to be taken as anything other than friendly support, and it especially wouldn't do to have Annie witness such a tender sign of affection should she peek out of the buggy.

"Just be who *Gott* created you to be," she finally suggested, choosing to offer verbal encouragement instead. "Trust that He knew exactly what He was doing when He made you. After all, He doesn't make any mistakes, *jah*?"

Aaron stopped in his tracks as if struck by her sentiment. "I never thought of it that way." He stared down at his worn boots. "*Denki* for saying such a *wunderbaar* thing." When he raised his gaze, his brown eyes were full of sweetness and warmth, reminding Grace of a mug of hot cocoa on a chilly winter day. "I'm glad you came to Bird-in-Hand."

Grace beamed at that. "I'm glad that *Daadi* guilted us into spending time together," she said with a chuckle, hoping that Aaron would appreciate the humor behind her sentiment.

Aaron startled, his eyes growing to the size of watermelons as his mouth dropped open. "W-what do you mean?"

Grace was bewildered by the sudden change in his disposition. "*Ach*, it was only a joke. We weren't keen on spending time together at first, *jah*?"

Still visibly unsettled, Aaron paused before bobbing his head. "I suppose so."

"Is everything *oll recht*?"

Before Aaron could reply, Annie's upbeat voice rang through the air.

"What's taking you two so long?" the girl called as she peeked out of the back of the buggy. "Are we gonna get goin' soon?"

"*Jah, jah*," Aaron said with a strained smile. "We ran into *aendi* Sarah and stopped to chat with her," he explained as he hurried over to the buggy. He placed the shopping bags in the back of the rig, then made his way to the hitching post and began to untie his horse.

What just happened? Had she said something wrong? Grace worried about Aaron's shift in mood as she climbed into the buggy and waited for him to join her on the front seat. Annie began telling Grace about the books she'd just purchased, as well as how excited she was to start reading them, but Grace barely heard a word Aaron's little sister said.

Aaron's bizarre reaction to her lighthearted comment about feeling forced to spend time together perplexed Grace, and she wondered why he suddenly seemed so uneasy. Why would a silly comment about them being set up for a shopping trip cause him to go as pale as fresh cow's milk?

Monday morning came with cloudy skies, downpours, and rumbles of thunder in the distance, though the gloomy weather didn't stop Aaron from arriving to work promptly at eight o'clock. After unhitching his horse and settling it in the stable, he dashed through the puddles and burst into the woodshop, where conditions were much more comfortable.

Eli was sitting at the metal desk in the far corner of the small building, shuffling around several carbon copies of receipts that he'd written for customers. Hearing the shop's door bang open, he jumped, took a good, long look at Aaron, then let out a deep cackle.

"It's a *gut* day to be a duck, *jah*?"

"I'd say so," Aaron said with a smirk. He glanced down at his rain-dampened clothing, the motion of his head causing a deluge of water droplets to fall from the brim of his straw hat. He chuckled at his predicament as he hung his hat on a hook, hoping that both the hat and his clothing would dry out quickly. "What should I get to work on first?"

"You tell me since you're running things now," Eli said as he tucked the receipts into the pocket of a blue folder. "But first, tell me about your weekend. How did everything go?"

"It was fine, I guess." Aaron hoped that Eli would accept the vague answer. He was certain that Eli was inquiring about his outing with Grace, and that wasn't a topic he was ready to approach. He'd enjoyed getting to know her better, and he genuinely appreciated the gentle way that she encouraged him to come out of his shell. Yet if he divulged this sentiment, Eli might misunderstand and assume that he and Grace were on their way to becoming close friends, and that certainly wasn't the case.

"If I remember correctly, we have an order for a dining

room table that needs to be finished by Thursday. We should finish sanding it so we can start staining it this afternoon," Aaron declared with a slight wavering in his voice, hoping the change in subject would go over well.

"*Ach*, it can wait. Tell me how things went with Grace on Saturday," Eli insisted, his deeply wrinkled face beaming with anticipation.

"It went well. My *schweschder*, Annie, came along with us," Aaron said as he picked up a new sheet of sandpaper and made his way to the table, which had only been partially sanded. "The three of us had a *gut* time, and *gut* conversation too. I think Annie is hoping that Grace will stay in Bird-in-Hand indefinitely." He tried to fight the grin that ached to spread across his lips but lost the battle. Privately, he also hoped that Grace would stick around.

"That's *wunderbaar* to hear," Eli said as he stood with great effort and reached for the cane that he'd recently started using. "I was thinking that—"

His words were interrupted by the sound of a small bell jingling from the next room.

"Sounds like your first customer is here." Eli slowly made his way toward the front of the building, where a small showroom was located. He paused, realizing that Aaron wasn't following him. "Are you coming?"

"*Jah*." Aaron gulped and followed Eli to the showroom, each step forward adding to his mounting anxiety. He'd like nothing more than to stay behind the scenes and focus on crafting beautiful furniture, but if he didn't test his people and business skills, Eli would find someone else to take over the woodshop.

As they rounded the corner, Aaron saw a smartly dressed *Englisch* man who looked to be in his mid-fifties.

The man turned when he heard Eli and Aaron enter the showroom and offered them a cheerful smile.

"Good morning, gentlemen. Who do I talk to about ordering a custom piece as an anniversary gift for my wife?" the man asked as he stepped forward.

Eli said nothing but turned his attention to Aaron. He gave his young employee an expectant look.

"That's me," Aaron said after mustering every ounce of courage within himself. "What do you want?" He cringed, hearing the tone of his words. "I mean, what type of piece were you looking to have made?"

The man pointed to a nearby rocking chair that was on display. Its dark varnish shone in the light of the battery-powered lanterns that hung from hooks on the ceiling. "I was hoping to give her something like that, though maybe in a different color."

"Did you just want a lighter stain or would you prefer to have it painted to match the walls in your home?" Aaron asked, trying not to look down at his trembling hands. Hopefully, the customer didn't notice just how nervous he was.

The *Englisch* man chewed on his tongue. "That's a good question." He hemmed and hawed as he glanced around the room. "What would you suggest?"

Aaron hung his head. He didn't enjoy being put on the spot and was especially uninterested in making decisions for someone else. What if he suggested something that sounded good in theory, but would ultimately disappoint the customer when he laid eyes on the final piece?

Eli started tapping his foot, letting Aaron know that he shouldn't keep the customer in suspense any longer.

"I've always been partial to a light honey-colored stain

with a glossy varnish," Aaron finally declared, lifting his gaze and speaking as steadily as he could. "The light color is cheerful in the summer and warm in the winter."

The customer bobbed his head, his smile returning. "That sounds good, really good. Would you be able to have it ready before September first?"

"I think so, but let me check on the orders we received earlier." Aaron hurried across the room, nearly tripping over his bootlaces that had become untied. Feeling his face flame with embarrassment, he took a seat behind the desk and shuffled through the list of pending orders. He confirmed that they could have the chair ready for pickup by September first, then invited the customer to take the empty chair on the opposite side of the desk. Aaron wrote down all the details of the order, then carefully went over the pricing for the project, doing the math mentally three times before sharing the rate with the customer. The man agreed to the price, signed the order slip, paid a deposit on the piece, then shook hands with Aaron.

"One more thing," Aaron called to the man as the man headed for the exit.

The customer spun around. "Yes?"

"I…uh… I was thinking that since the rocker will be an anniversary gift, maybe you'd like me to carve your initials, and your wife's, onto the rocker's crest rail," Aaron suggested. He was still flushed from the unspoken pressure of the interaction. "W-would you like that?"

"Would it cost extra?"

"*Nee*… I mean, no. That would be my gift to your family…if you'd like to have it done."

The *Englisch* man's face lit up. "That would be excellent! Thank you so much for your thoughtfulness." He provided the initials to be carved into the rocker. "I'll see you in a couple of weeks." With that, he headed out of the showroom.

Aaron let out a pent-up exhale.

"That went well, *jah*?" Eli said cheerfully as he lowered himself into the chair that the customer had just vacated.

Aaron shook his head as he added a note about the initials on the order slip. "I was a wreck. First I was short with the customer. Then I tripped over my own feet." He added the order slip to the stack of current projects, then dragged his hands down his face. "I was so *naerfich* that I gave myself a stomachache."

"But you also took care of his needs, made a suggestion he liked, and made him feel like we valued his business. Those are the most important things," Eli countered. "This was a *wunderbaar gut* first step, and if you keep this up, you'll be ready to take over the business in no time."

"I don't know," Aaron said with a groan as he stood and plodded back to the woodshop. "Maybe I can't handle this. I'm just too awkward and *naerfich* around folks I don't know."

"You were also *naerfich* about your outing with Gracie," Eli said as he followed Aaron, his pace slower and his gait slightly unsteady. "Look how well that turned out."

"It did go well, but that's only because of Grace," Aaron replied. He felt his heart skip a beat as an image of her lovely smile floated into his mind. "She's exceptionally understanding, kind, funny, and…"

Aaron stopped talking when he heard Eli's footsteps come to a halt. He spun around to see Eli staring at him with an eager, nearly jovial grin.

"And?" Eli asked, his gray eyebrows rising so high that they nearly disappeared beneath his straw hat.

"I just mean that she's really...she's..."

Eli let out a chuckle so powerful that it bounced off the woodshop's walls, echoing like the clanging of a mighty iron bell.

"Eli, please don't get any ideas about this," Aaron begged as Eli brushed past him, still laughing gleefully. "I just meant that Grace is—"

"I know exactly what you meant, *yung* man," Eli said at the end of a chuckle, interrupting Aaron's sentiment. "Now, let's get back to work before you say anything else."

Chapter Six

Things fell into a comfortable pattern for Grace as time marched on. After fixing breakfast for herself and her grandfather around seven o'clock each morning, she spent the rest of her mornings deep-cleaning the cottage, one room at a time. When it was time for the noon meal, she fixed a light lunch for Eli, Aaron, and herself, then took the food out to the woodshop and enjoyed the meal break with the men. She soon grew fond of the time spent reconnecting with Eli and strengthening her friendship with Aaron.

Her afternoons were spent mending Eli's clothes, tending to his small vegetable garden, and caring for the needs of Eli's chestnut-colored mare, Rosie. When time allowed, she enjoyed sitting on the back porch with a glass of meadow tea and her journal, writing down daily happenings and her thoughts and she listened to the babble of nearby Mill Creek and the gentle fluttering of the cottage's colorful quilts as they aired on the clothesline.

One sunny Tuesday afternoon, Grace found herself walking back and forth across the front lawn behind her grandfather's rotary lawn mower. Now that the recent humid spell had passed, the warmth of the sun felt good against her face and forearms, and she quite enjoyed being outdoors. She paused to inhale the sweet, summery scent of fresh-cut grass, relishing the opportunity to enjoy one of her favorite aromas.

She couldn't recall the last time she'd stopped to enjoy life's simple pleasures, or "love notes from *Gott*," as her grandfather liked to call the small daily moments of comfort. Truly, she'd consumed herself with constant business and distractions ever since being jilted, yet the past two weeks she'd spent in Bird-in-Hand had been the perfect remedy for what ailed her. Perhaps it was the change of scenery that felt like a balm to her soul, or maybe it was the presence of her wise grandfather. Though she thought it unlikely, maybe her newfound, unassuming friendship with Aaron King was also putting some pep back into her.

Grace finished mowing the final strip of grass and then decided to check the mailbox before fixing lunch. She opened the lid to the metal box, peeked inside, and was greeted by a hefty stack of mail. Along with some advertisements for a local candle shop, a flier about the hot air balloon festival that would take place in a few weeks, and a letter from her father to Eli, Grace was intrigued to discover two envelopes that were addressed to her.

Plagued with curiosity, she made her way to a nearby oak tree and took a seat on the ground beneath it, enjoying the shade that the dense covering of leaves provided. She placed the stack of mail to her right, then examined the first envelope with her name on it. She noticed the name Abby Esh penned neatly in the return address. The letter was from her older married sister, and Grace was eager to read what her favorite sibling had written.

She removed a greeting card from the envelope and admired the lovely bouquet of sunflowers that were pictured on the front, along with the words "Thinking of You" in large golden letters. Grace opened the card and read the handwritten message inside.

Dearest Grace,
Just writing to let you know that you are in my daily thoughts, and I'm praying that the Lord will use your time in Bird-in-Hand for healing. I'm counting the hours until you, and *Daadi*, return to us.
Your loving *schweschder*,
Abby

Grace chewed on her tongue as she closed the card, then studied the sunflower field that was featured on its front, wishing that she felt as cheerful as the blossoms appeared to be. While she truly appreciated her sister's kind sentiment, Grace could read between the lines. Here was yet another reminder of her lost love. How was she supposed to heal if people kept bringing up her miserably failed relationship? Every mention of her broken heart, no matter how well-intentioned, reminded her of what she desperately longed to forget.

Placing the pretty card on top of the stack of Eli's mail, Grace reached for the second envelope that was addressed to her. The return address listed the name of her closest friend, Lizzie Lapp, which brought a smile back to Grace's lips. Knowing Lizzie went out of her way to find Eli's address, Grace eagerly tore open the envelope and pulled out a sheet of pretty pink stationery. Her eyes ran along the perfectly straight lines of impeccable penmanship.

Hello, Grace!
How are you enjoying your time spent in Bird-in-Hand? I'm sure that your *grossdaadi* loves having

you around, though I'm missing my best friend something fierce! Have you had a chance to do anything fun or make any new friends?

I've been keeping busy working in my parents' bookstore, as usual, though I did recently attend a picnic for the *die youngie* of Paradise and Strasburg. We had ourselves a real *gut* time, and I wish you could have been there. It's always good for the soul to meet new folks.

I better sign off for now and help fix supper. Write back to me soon, and tell me all about your time in Bird-in-Hand.

Fondly,

Lizzie Lapp

Grace finished reading Lizzie's letter and let out a groan. It was clear that her bubbly, thoughtful friend was attempting to convince her to give courting another chance. Why else would she mention a youth event, as well as the notion of meeting new people?

She blinked against the tears that were filling her eyes. Just when she'd finally started enjoying daily life again, here came not one, but two reminders of her former beau and his betrayal.

How were her raw wounds ever supposed to heal if they continued to be torn open? Why couldn't others accept that courtship and marriage just weren't meant for her? Would she spend the rest of her life with constant reminders that she'd missed out on her chance to be loved?

Grace was overwhelmed with unpleasant emotions, some of which stirred from a deep loneliness in her heart. Other negative feelings stemmed from the fact that no one, not even her closest sister or best friend, understood how she felt. Giving into the grief that had once again reared its ugly head, Grace tossed Lizzie's letter to the side, cradled her head in her palms, and let her tears flow.

"Yow!"

Aaron had been sweeping up a pile of sawdust off the woodshop floor when he heard a sickening whack followed by Eli's yelp. He spun around just in time to see Eli drop the hammer that he'd been holding and then give his left thumb a tight squeeze.

"This is what I get for thinking I didn't need my glasses," Eli said through gritted teeth as pain etched across his face.

Aaron leaned the broom against the closest workbench and then darted to Eli's side. "Are you *oll recht*? You didn't break your thumb, did you?"

"*Nee*, just smashed it real *gut*." He slowly wiggled the injured thumb and let out a whistle. "That was a real wake-up call. I better go fetch my glasses before I end up with two sore thumbs."

Aaron chuckled, relieved that Eli wasn't severely injured and was in good spirits. "I'll go get them for you. Where will I find them?"

"I think I left them at the table when I finished breakfast," Eli said as he stooped to pick up the hammer that he'd dropped. "Feel free to take a little break if you'd like to do so. I'm going to sit down until my thumb quits throbbing."

Aaron thanked Eli, then moseyed out of the woodshop and made his way toward the cottage. He walked across the lawn, taking the time to stretch and take a few deep breaths of the fresh country air, which didn't feel nearly as sticky as it had in the past few weeks.

As he traipsed toward the cottage he suddenly halted and stood perfectly still. Was that a woman crying? He held his breath and glanced around for the source of the faint whimpering that he was certain he'd heard. He searched beyond the cottage and spotted Grace seated in the shade of a towering oak tree, weeping into her hands.

Aaron's mouth went dry as he wondered what to do. His first reaction was to scurry into the cottage before he could be spotted. Grace probably wanted her privacy. She might feel embarrassed if caught having an emotional moment.

On second thought, sympathy for his new friend weighed heavy on his conscience. It pained him to see anyone upset, especially someone he cared about.

Did he care for Grace? He questioned himself as he stood frozen in place. Of course, as one friend would care for another.

Unsure of what he would say to the distraught woman, Aaron decided that he could not stand by and let Grace cry without offering her some support. He headed toward the tree and hoped that Grace wouldn't think that he'd been spying on her. As he approached, he cleared his throat to announce his presence.

Grace looked up, her cheeks flushed and tear-streaked. "*Ach*, Aaron." She put her hand against her chest. "You startled me."

"Sorry. That's exactly what I was trying to avoid." He squatted down to be at her eye level. "I…uh… I noticed that you were…"

Grace sniffled and let out a pained chuckle. "I'm embarrassed. I must look like a mess."

"Not at all," Aaron replied sincerely. He hesitated as she dabbed at her eyes. "Are you *oll recht*?"

"I don't know." She looked away from him and stared at a pile of papers and envelopes that rested in the grass beside her.

Filled with pity, Aaron dropped to his knees, crawled up to Grace, and took a seat in the grass beside her. "Is there anything that I can do to help?"

Still refusing to look at him, Grace shook her head. "Only if you want to hear me complain for a while."

"Sure, I'd love to." Aaron wanted to smack himself in the face, mortified by his own choice of words. Hopefully, Grace wouldn't think he was desperate for her attention. Yet his concern for her overshadowed his embarrassment, and he inched closer to her side. "Tell me, *wass iss letz*?"

Grace turned her head to face him, the movement causing a fresh round of tears to spill down her cheeks. "It's a long story."

Aaron gave a small, encouraging grin. "I've got time."

Grace took a very long, very deep breath. "I had a beau until recently. We were together for seven years."

Aaron nodded but kept silent, thinking of how terribly long a seven-year courtship seemed. Most couples tied the knot after two or three years of courting.

But who was he to judge? It wasn't like he had any experience with courting, Aaron firmly reminded himself.

"Things didn't work out between him and me," Grace continued, her voice heavy with melancholy. Her shoulders slumped so severely that it was a wonder how she didn't topple over.

"W-what happened?"

Grace offered a pained smile through her tears, which were starting to slow. "That's a story for another day."

"I understand. Don't say it if you can't," Aaron replied,

though his curiosity was nearly as overwhelming as a litter of untrained puppies.

"*Denki*," Grace replied, the tip of her nose nearly as red as a cherry. "Anyway, I don't want to think about love or marriage ever again, yet I'm constantly bombarded with reminders." She looked up at the cloudless blue sky and then scoffed. "I thought a change of scenery would help, but even here in Bird-in-Hand, I'm still a prisoner of the past."

Aaron's lips drooped into a frown. He was deeply affected by his friend's words, and the sorrowful look on her freckled face. "What's keeping you from moving on?"

Grace let out a puff and then gestured to the pile of mail, beside her. "My *familye* and *freind* keep pushing me to move on." She paused, pulling a dainty floral handkerchief out of her dress sleeve, and then wiped away the moisture from her face. "Their intentions are *gut*, I'm sure of that, but constantly suggesting that I open my heart again isn't helping me forget that it's been broken. How am I ever supposed to move on if I'm not allowed time to heal?"

"I've never been in *lieb*, but I can imagine how it would feel to be pressured into an uncomfortable situation," Aaron responded, feeling as heavy as an August storm cloud. As he observed Grace's melancholy demeanor, he felt an overwhelming need to comfort her. What could he do, what could he say, that might take her mind off of her heartbreak?

Suddenly an idea popped into his mind. "There's a work frolic coming up this Saturday," he said. "It's gonna be at Samuel Fisher's farm. They have over two acres of blueberry bushes, and the berries are ripening faster than they can pick them. A lot of folks from our church district will be going to help. Would…would you like to go with me?"

Grace's turquoise eyes were suddenly as wide as the brim of Aaron's straw hat. "You want me to go with you?"

Aaron hadn't initially planned on attending the work frolic since social situations weren't his favorite thing. But if attending the event would help Grace to cheer up, he'd happily go.

"*Jah*, I'm thinking that it would be a nice time for both of us. You can get to know some of the folks around here, and there will be no pressure to pair off for courting since it's a family event," he explained, hoping that Grace understood his intentions. He felt somewhat lightheaded, surprised at his sudden boldness.

Grace continued to stare at him with her mouth slightly agape.

"You could even write back to your sister and friend and tell them that you went to a work frolic with me," he went on, feeling his heart start to pound. "They might take the hint and stop bringing up…well, you know."

He glanced away from her, overcome with embarrassment. Why had he assumed that Grace would want to be seen at the work frolic with him, or tell others that she'd attended with him? He was infamous for saying the wrong thing at the wrong time, and he hoped with all of his being that this wasn't one of those occasions. Perhaps his suggestion was even insensitive.

A warm smile spread across Grace's lips, which lit up her face like the glow of a lantern. "*Denki* for your kindness, Aaron." She reached over and placed her hand on top of his. "It means a lot to me, and I'd love to attend the work frolic." She gave his hand a quick squeeze. "I can't remember the last time I looked forward to something."

Aaron glanced down at Grace's hand, still on top of his. His heart raced at her gentle touch, a sensation that was unfamiliar, both pleasant and terrifying at the same time.

Startled by the fluttering through his soul, he sprung to his feet, pulling his hand from beneath hers. "I… I better get back to work. Eli might think that I somehow got myself lost."

Grace giggled, shielding her grin with her slender hand. "Okay." She stood, though her rising was much more poised than Aaron's had been. "I'll see you around lunchtime."

"Right. See you then." Feeling more than a little flustered, he spun around and hurried off to the woodshop.

What just happened? Aaron dashed across the lawn in disbelief at what had just occurred. Grace's innocent touch had nearly taken his breath away. What a reaction he'd had to her tears, and to the tender way that she'd clasped his hand! True, he'd never been the calm, collected type, but the intensity of his reaction to their exchange startled him deeply.

Am I interested in Grace? He already knew the answer to that question.

Determined to think of something else, Aaron focused his attention on the woodshop, which he'd nearly reached, then halted. He'd forgotten to find Eli's glasses. He spun around to head back to the cottage and was surprised to see Grace sprinting toward him.

"Is everything *oll recht*?" he asked, hustling forward to meet her.

"*Jah*, I just figured you'd be looking for these." She held up her hand to reveal Eli's bifocals.

Aaron gently took the glasses from her. "How'd you know I'd be looking for these?"

Grace lifted her shoulders in an endearing shrug. "I just had a feeling," she replied as her warm smile lit up her eyes.

There it was again, that unfamiliar rush of delightful jitters that Aaron experienced more and more frequently when Grace was around. Heat rushed to his face, so much so that his eyes nearly started to water.

Grace's knowing smile grew broader as if amused by Aaron's sudden blush. "I…uh… I saw that *Daadi* left his glasses on the table after breakfast this morning and I assumed one of you would come looking for them." She pressed her lips together, suppressing an obvious chortle that ached to be released.

Though he'd normally be riddled with embarrassment to be caught blushing, this time Aaron didn't feel an ounce of shame. His little smirk morphed into a full-blown smile, which then turned into a bout of chuckles.

Grace joined in on the merriment, and soon the two friends were nearly winded from their peals of laughter.

Aaron thanked Grace for bringing Eli's glasses and they parted ways. As he approached the woodshop for a second time, his grin remained steady, so much so that his cheeks started to ache. Grace certainly brought out the best in him, and that was a difficult feat.

It doesn't matter. Just because Grace and I are friends doesn't mean that she'd be interested in courting me.

His smile disappeared as quickly as autumn leaves on a gusty day. He plodded into the woodshop, made his way over to Eli, and handed him the glasses.

"*Denki*, Aaron." Eli grinned as he dawned his spectacles. "I can always count on you." Pressing his palm against the nearby workbench, he took his time standing up. "We better get back to work so we don't fall behind on our orders."

Aaron agreed and went to find a dustpan to clean up the pile of sawdust he'd swept earlier before moving on to the next project. As he knelt to sweep up the dusty mess into the pan, Eli's words echoed through his mind.

"I can always count on you."

Aaron rose when the pan was filled, then dumped the pan's contents into a nearby trash bin. Could Eli really count on him? Aaron questioned himself as he peeked over his shoulder at his elderly employer. Eli had asked him to run the shop, and the thought of it scared him half to death. He'd also been asked to befriend Grace, not start to develop feelings for her. If he couldn't be trusted to do what he was asked, he probably shouldn't be trusted to take over Eli's business.

Chapter Seven

Saturday morning dawned with plenty of sunshine and a gentle breeze, the ideal weather for an outdoor work frolic. Aaron and his horse and buggy arrived promptly at eight-fifteen to collect Grace. The pair arrived at the expansive Fisher farm about twenty minutes later.

Grace stood beside Aaron's buggy as he unhitched his horse and walked it to the pasture, where Clove could mingle with the other visiting horses, graze on lush grass, and drink from the narrow stream that snaked through the meadow. She glanced toward the farmhouse where a large cluster of women gathered around a long folding table, seemingly setting up some refreshments. Several small groups of men, some with beards and some clean-shaven, talked and laughed together near the enormous white barn. Groups of children were dotted across the lawn, some playing tag, some whispering secrets, and others playing patty-cake.

"Ready to go pick a few berries?" Aaron called over his shoulder as he closed the gate to the fenced-in pasture.

"I am," Grace replied with a grin, "although I think we'll be picking more than a few berries today."

"By the time we're through, we may pick over a dozen pounds each," Aaron said as they headed toward the gathering. "The plan is to pick every last berry from the bushes, and there are a lot of bushes."

"*Vell* then, we'll pick until our pickers are sore," Grace declared.

They both laughed at that comment.

Grace inhaled the morning air, still cool and damp from the night before. The lovely weather helped her to feel relaxed and hopeful. It had been far too long since she had something to look forward to, and she could already feel her spirits climbing out of the swampy gloom that she'd been stuck in for months.

She peered over at Aaron and noticed that he was wearing a white Sunday shirt. That was very unusual, especially for a day that would be spent picking berries, which could potentially leave a noticeable purple stain if accidentally squished.

Aaron caught Grace looking at him, then looked down at his shirt. "Just wanted to make a *gut* impression today," he sheepishly admitted.

"But don't you already know most of the folks who will be here?"

"*Jah*, but I don't socialize often," he shrugged in response. "I guess I'm a little *naerfich*."

"I should be the *naerfich* one," Grace said as she stopped to pet the playful golden retriever that had just bounded up to them. "I'm the one meeting new people."

"*Ach*, you've got nothing to be *naerfich* about," Aaron answered as he took his turn petting the dog's silky head. "Everyone's real nice, and you've already met a handful of them at church."

"Then why are you *naerfich*?" Grace questioned, raising one of her eyebrows.

"Must be a force of habit," Aaron answered, causing them both to chuckle.

The friendly dog led Grace and Aaron to the rest of the volunteers, and Grace was nearly moved to tears by the warm welcome that she received. She quickly learned that some of the workers were members of the Fisher family, some attended the same church district, and others were simply friends and neighbors. Lydia Beachy, a young woman around Grace's age, greeted Grace with a warm embrace. Nancy Riehl, a middle-aged widow, invited Grace to come to her house to have some tea. Hannah Yoder, a plump, red-haired woman encouraged Grace to reach out to her anytime that she needed help while tending to things around Eli's cottage. Even Diane Stolar, an Englisch neighbor of the Fishers, greeted Grace with enthusiastic hospitality.

Grace scanned the small crowd and easily spotted Aaron as he stood near some other young men, the brightness of his shirt nearly sending out a beacon among the various shades of blue, gray, and green that the other men wore. Her heart was warmed when she noticed that his peers were attempting to include Aaron in their conversation. Though he kept his gaze mostly fixed on his boots and only spoke when directly addressed, Grace thought he might be on the verge of coming out of his shell.

"Grace Ebersol? Is that you?"

Grace spun around and her mouth dropped open. There was Lizzie Lapp, her dearest friend, and Lizzie's twin brother, Luke. It came as a shock to see the tall, slender, Lapp siblings here in Bird-in-Hand.

"I can't believe it," Lizzie exclaimed as she rushed over and wrapped Grace in a warm, sisterly embrace. "If I'd gone one more day without seeing you, I might've forgotten what you looked like."

Grace laughed as she held her closest friend. "*Ach*, it hasn't been all that long, but I sure am glad to see both of you." When she and Lizzie finally released each other, she turned to Luke and shook his outstretched hand.

"A month can feel like an awful long time when you're separated from someone you care about," Luke said, his suntanned face shining as brightly as the morning sun. "Lizzie's been talking about you nonstop since you left Paradise."

Grace smiled broadly, feeling very cherished by her friends. "I'm *eckseidt* to see both of you! What are you doing here, though?"

"This is our cousin's farm," Lizzie answered, gesturing to the gigantic barn behind them. "We've come to help pick berries."

"Did you think we came looking for you and just happened to find you here?" Luke asked with a mischievous grin.

Grace snickered when Lizzie not-so-gently elbowed her brother in the ribs.

"It looks like you have a friend that we've never met," Lizzie said as she gestured to someone behind Grace.

Grace glanced over her shoulder and saw Aaron approaching with a cautious grin. Had she left him in the dust when she'd run to greet her friends, or had he purposely held back, perhaps feeling a little nervous, or maybe to allow her some private time to reconnect? She was struck by the sight of him, dressed in his best clothes and clearly unable to hide his apprehension.

"This is Aaron King," Grace made the introduction as

Aaron stepped up to her side. "He's my new *freind* and the sole employee at my *daadi*'s woodshop." She gave him what she hoped was a reassuring smile.

Lizzie and Luke exchanged glances that were a mixture of surprise and amusement.

"*G-guder mariye*," Aaron quietly stammered, nodding first at Lizzie and then at Luke.

Smiling, Grace looked down and noticed Aaron's trembling hand, just inches from her own. How easy it would be to simply take his hand in hers and give it a squeeze of comfort, but doing so would certainly raise the eyebrows of her friends, and anyone else who might be watching.

"It's *gut* to meet you, Aaron," Luke chirped. He extended his hand to Aaron, and when Aaron accepted it, he gave it a firm shake that must have taken Aaron off guard. Aaron stepped forward unsteadily, nearly losing his balance.

"It's *very* nice to meet you," Lizzie emphasized, also shaking Aaron's hand after he'd regained his balance.

"I'm glad to meet some of Grace's friends from Paradise," Aaron said with a reserved grin, the volume of his voice increasing ever so slightly.

Grace sensed that Aaron was starting to feel a little more comfortable and considered how she could help boost his confidence. "Aaron will be a *wunderbaar* help today because he's a hard worker. He puts so much care into his work that *Daadi* has recently asked Aaron to take over his business."

Aaron turned as red as a ripe strawberry when Lizzie and Luke oohed and aahed over the momentous news, but his timid smile never disappeared.

"You must be having a *wunderbaar gut* summer then,

jah, Aaron? You've got yourself a new business and a new girlfriend," Luke said, splitting a playfully mischievous look between Aaron and Grace.

Lizzie inhaled sharply as an unmistakable glint of hope flashed across her face. "Is that true, Grace? When did you two start courting?"

"You were supposed to be helping your *daadi* during your visit to Bird-in-Hand, not find yourself a beau," Luke teased as he winked dramatically at Grace.

Grace felt her heart leap into her throat and become lodged there, like a massive boulder in a trickling creek. She hadn't expected her friends to come right out and ask if she and Aaron were courting, especially right in front of his face. She'd hoped that his presence alone would satisfy their curiosities about her romantic life. As she looked at the optimistic, eager faces of her friends, she found herself in a terrible pickle. She couldn't lie to Lizzie and Luke, yet she didn't have the energy it would take to have this familiar conversation once again. If she had to explain her stance on courtship, and the fact that she refused to risk emotional devastation for a second time, she would surely succumb to a puddle of tears. Perhaps it had been a mistake to attend the frolic after all.

"*Jah*, I've certainly got a lot going on right now," Aaron spoke up, interrupting Grace's internal panic. "Lots of new things. Lots of *gut* things."

Grace stared at Aaron as relief washed over her like a cool rain shower. He'd mercifully rescued her from digging up painful emotions that were better off remaining buried. He'd also willingly put himself in the spotlight, which was a place that Grace knew he'd rather avoid. He'd done all this for her.

"We can all use more *gut* things," Lizzie replied, seemingly having accepted Aaron's vague explanation. "Let's go see what kind of goodies the Fishers have for us," she suggested, adding to Grace's relief.

"You don't have to ask me twice," Luke added, giving his stomach a few pats before making a beeline toward the table of refreshments.

Lizzie rolled her eyes, shook her head, and followed her twin brother.

Grace and Aaron walked behind Lizzie, though neither of them said anything. She looked over at the tall, handsome fellow who was walking beside her, still recovering from the shock of how he'd instinctively come to her aid.

He must have felt her eyes on him. He looked over at her and offered a subtle grin.

"*Denki*," Grace silently mouthed, hoping he would understand.

Aaron bobbed his head and gave her a wink.

Grace couldn't help but consider what a fine beau, or even husband, Aaron would make for some special woman. Sure, he was a little rough around the edges, but his awkwardness didn't outshine his gentle, understanding spirit. She knew that if her heart was willing, she could easily fall for Aaron King. Yet with Aaron's cute mannerisms, caring nature, and rugged good looks, Grace knew that she would need to guard her heart with the utmost vigilance to keep that from happening. Having experienced heartbreak once was enough for a lifetime and she would not risk going through that pain ever again.

After everyone had arrived, the team of about thirty Amish people and a few *Englischers* made their way to the blueberry field. Aaron was impressed by the dozens of perfectly straight rows of bushes, and upon seeing the size of the task at hand, he understood why the Fishers had called upon their friends and neighbors for help with the harvesting.

Tin pails were handed out to everyone, then two workers were assigned to each row of bushes. Workers were instructed to pick the bush clean of every ripe berry before moving on to the next bush. Large ten-gallon tin tubs were placed on the ground between every seven or so bushes. Once the workers filled their pails with berries, they gingerly dumped their harvest into the larger tubs before they started to fill their pails again.

Aaron thoroughly enjoyed the morning spent in the blueberry field. Though he was his usual bashful self, he still felt included in conversation by those who were nearby. He enjoyed listening to their humorous anecdotes and was especially pleased to hear the musical sound of Grace's laughter as she talked with some of the women who'd readily accepted her. Aaron also relished popping the occasional handful of berries into his mouth, delighting in the sweet, juicy flavor, just as all of the workers had been encouraged to do.

When it was time for the noon meal, nearly half of the blueberry bushes had been completely stripped of their berries. While the women went back to the house to prepare lunch, the men pulled together to bring the harvest in from the fields.

Aaron teamed up with fun-loving Luke Lapp. Luke sat in the wagon and manned the reins, guiding the enormous tan draft horse while Aaron effortlessly lifted the heavy tin tubs into the back of the wagon.

"You're a quiet fellow, aren't you, Aaron?"

"*Jah*, that's true," Aaron answered as he hoisted one of the tubs into the back of the wagon.

"Nothing wrong with that, though I sure would like to know what you're thinking."

Aaron chuckled at Luke's polite directness. "I was thinking that I've never seen so many blueberries in my life." He pointed at the growing load in the wagon bed. "There are more berries here than there are at the farmers' market, and we're not even halfway done picking."

Luke turned from his seat on the wagon's bench. "Are you talking about Lancaster Central Market, the Green Dragon Market, Roots Market, or the Bird-in-Hand Farmers' Market?"

"Doesn't matter," Aaron replied with a shy grin. "There are more berries here than at all of those markets combined."

Now it was Luke's turn to chuckle. "So," he went on after clicking his tongue to get the horse moving, "you're into woodworking?"

"*Jah*, I've always liked building things ever since I was a *yung bu*," Aaron said as he walked alongside the wagon, listening to the creaking of its iron wheels as they slowly turned. "I worked for a Mennonite construction company when I was a teen, but I enjoy my current job of crafting furniture much more."

"And soon you'll be running the business," Luke said, with a bright smile that illuminated his hazel eyes.

"*Jah*, but there's no guarantee that I'll take over for Eli when he retires," Aaron replied, watching the horse's head as it bobbed up and down with each and every slow step. "There's more to running a woodshop than just carpentry."

Luke pulled on the reins and brought the horse to a halt before turning to shoot Aaron a questioning look.

"You know, there's keeping the books, ordering supplies, and dealing with customers," Aaron said as he headed for the next tub of berries.

"Right," Luke responded, "but I don't see why that would be an issue."

Aaron grunted as he lifted the container of berries, which seemed to be the heaviest one yet. He let out a puff of air as he placed the tub in the wagon. "Eli wants me to prove that I can handle all that, and I don't know if I can."

Luke's carefree smile melted into a thoughtful expression. "I've been to Eli's woodshop to pick up a hope chest that was a gift for Lizzie, and it was a downright pleasant experience."

"You probably were helped by Eli." Aaron hung his head. "I'd have messed something up, charged you an incorrect price, or sent you home with the wrong hope chest."

Luke turned around in his seat and stared at Aaron while wearing a concerned frown. "Why are you so hard on yourself? Eli wouldn't have asked you to take over for him if he didn't think you were the right man for the job. It sounds like this trial period he's putting you through is so you can prove to *yourself* that you're more than capable."

Aaron stared down at his work boots, noticing a small purple stain where a squashed berry must've fallen on his left shoe. He'd never considered that the probation period might have been for his benefit, but it would be just like wise Eli to come up with such a plan.

Luke clicked his tongue and the horse started forward

again. The rattling of the tin tubs against each other interrupted Aaron's thoughts but before he could respond, Luke spoke up again.

"Not to change the subject, but are you and Grace courting? You two didn't give me and Lizzie a clear answer earlier."

Aaron's face burned with heat, though he knew it wasn't from spending his entire morning in the August sun. "I…uh…you see…"

Luke threw his head back and guffawed. His straw hat tumbled off his blond head and landed on top of a heap of berries. "That answers that question." He continued chuckling as Aaron hurried past the horse, making his escape toward the last tub of berries that needed to be collected. "Do you *want* to court Grace?"

"Of course I would," Aaron responded gruffly, knowing this answer stemmed from both his desire and his promise to Eli that he would warm up to the young woman. "What *yung* man wouldn't be interested in her?"

Luke remained silent until Aaron loaded the last tub of berries into the bed, climbed into the wagon, and took a seat beside him on the driver's bench. "Lots of *yung* men are interested in courting Grace." He looked to the left and then to the right, quietly observing their surroundings before he continued. "I can think of at least six single fellows, including myself, who've approached her and asked to take her out for ice cream or drive her home from a singing, but she's turned all of us down. She hasn't shown interest in anyone since her beau jilted her, but I think that's about to change."

Aaron's stomach dropped at the thought of anyone hurting Grace. "Why's that?"

Luke's grin returned as he signaled to the horse, who let out a whinny as she started moving forward. "Because she's smiling again. I noticed how she looks at you, and a *maedel* doesn't look at a guy with a twinkle in her eye unless she's interested in him."

Aaron sat motionless beside Luke as the horse pulled the wagon down the narrow dirt path that connected the blueberry fields to the other fields, as well as the barn. He felt stupefied by Luke's observation and had trouble finding any truth in it.

"It looks like you've won over both Eli and his *enkelin*, my friend," Luke declared, playfully nudging Aaron with his elbow while keeping a steady grip on the reins. "If you can do all that, you must be pretty special, so don't be so mean to yourself."

Before Aaron could respond, Luke brought the horse to a halt beside the barn, set the wagon's brake, then hopped to the ground. Several other men who were chatting near the barn came over to help unload the berries.

Aaron jumped down and joined the others in unloading the harvest, though his mind was not on the task, or the various conversations going on around him. His initial reaction was to brush off the compliments he'd received, but something about hearing such kind words from a practical stranger made them sticky like molasses in Aaron's mind. Maybe Luke was right. Maybe he did have a chance, even if it was as small as a field mouse, to win Grace's heart. Luke's words had given him an ounce of confidence, which was more than he'd ever had before, and it would be a shame to let the surge of courage go to waste.

When the time was right, he'd ask Grace if he could

court her, Aaron planned, grinning to himself as he concocted the idea. She'd probably turn him down, but something told him that he'd always regret it if he didn't take the risk.

Chapter Eight

By four o'clock that afternoon, every berry had been picked from the blueberry bushes, leaving time for relaxing and socializing. Some played volleyball and others seated themselves beneath shade trees to chat as the children splashed around in the nearby creek. The Fishers thanked everyone who had volunteered their time by serving a BBQ supper. Everyone enjoyed eating pulled pork sandwiches, macaroni salad, homemade potato chips, and several varieties of whoopie pies. When everyone had eaten their fill and visited some more, the Fishers sent each family home with a quart of blueberries as a token of thanks.

Just before sunset, Aaron and Grace set out for home. Aaron didn't rush Clove as the agreeable horse pulled the buggy down South Weavertown Road beneath a cloudless periwinkle sky.

Grace grinned to herself, enjoying the cool evening air and the rhythmic clip-clopping of the gelding's hooves. She glanced down at the twin quart containers that took up a spot on the buggy's seat between her and Aaron. She reached for her box and skimmed a few berries off the top, then popped them into her mouth.

"There's nothing more yummy than blueberries," she

declared as she took a second handful. "I think I'm going to make some blueberry pie with my share."

"My *mamm* will probably do the same...if Annie and my other siblings don't eat them all first," Aaron replied. "I may need to figure out a way to sneak into the *haus* and hide them so that doesn't happen."

Grace chuckled. "Sounds like a lot of folks will be glad that we attended the frolic, and I am too." She glanced out of the buggy at the sound of a whinny and her eyes landed on a spunky white foal who was standing behind a wire fence. The filly neighed a second greeting, then turned and trotted toward her mother who was grazing nearby. Grace realized that she felt nearly as content as the little horse sounded. Making new friends and forgetting her heartbreak, even if only temporarily, had done wonders for her spirit. "It's been a long time since I've had such a nice day," she said with a pleasant sigh. "I'm glad that I came with you."

"So am I," Aaron said heartily. He briefly took his eyes off the road to peer at Grace, his face flushing with color. He readjusted his grip on the reins, fidgeting with the leather ropes as if they were boot laces. "I usually don't attend community gatherings, other than church, of course. Now I'm thinking that maybe going to the next gathering for *die youngies* might not be such a bad thing."

Grace let out a mock gasp. "Don't tell me that you're turning into a social butterfly!"

"Nope, still just a caterpillar, but hopefully a less-isolated caterpillar."

Grace giggled at Aaron's uncharacteristically direct remark. "That's *gut* to hear because there are still lots of fun things that we can do together before the summer is over."

She shivered, surprised by her own enthusiasm. Sure, the pain of having been jilted by her only love still lingered, but it was no longer cemented in the front of her mind. Her new friends in Bird-in-Hand had breathed a spark of life into the damp kindling of her spirit. Truthfully, it had been Aaron who'd gotten the ball rolling for her, and she appreciated their blossoming friendship.

She looked over at the kind, quiet fellow beside her, admiring his meek ways. "I wanted to say *denki* for taking the pressure off of me when we ran into Lizzie and Luke," Grace stated, noticing that Aaron had managed to keep his white Sunday shirt free from stains, even after a day spent berry-picking. "They mean well and I love them both, but if I had to explain my stance on courting one more time, I think I'd just burst into tears."

Aaron turned the horse onto Harvest Drive and then gave a humble grin. "No thanks needed."

"Still, I appreciate what you did for me. Sometimes it seems like you are the only person who understands how I feel."

Aaron took his eyes off the road and they landed on Grace, his chiseled face filled with empathy. "I know what you mean. Everyone deserves to be understood."

Grace smiled graciously and Aaron beamed at her.

Aaron glanced down at her hands and his gaze lingered there for several seconds. When his eyes rose to meet hers again, he started to say something but was cut off when his horse let out a neigh and a snort. Aaron kept a firm, steady grip on the reins and spoke some soothing words to the gelding, ensuring that the animal hadn't been startled by something.

Grace sat silently, twiddling her thumbs and observing

Aaron. She could tell by the serious expression on his face that something important was on his mind.

"We've got a litter of *busslin* in our barn," Aaron said out of nowhere as his cheeks returned to their normal color. "Annie spends so much time with them that those kittens will grow up thinking she's their *mamm*."

"How sweet," Grace replied, nearly feeling whiplash from the sudden change in their conversation's topic. "I remember how exciting it was to have *busslin* on our farm when I was a little *maedel*."

"Annie really likes you, and I think she looks up to you too," he went on as the gentle breeze rustled his bowl-cut hair. "With only *brieder* for siblings, I think she wishes you were her big *schweschder*."

Grace made a small, happy sound, then turned her head to hide the tears that were forming in her eyes. She adored Aaron's little sister and was honored to hear that the darling girl thought so highly of her.

"Since tomorrow is an off-Sunday from church, I was wondering if you'd like to come over to our place to visit. Annie can show you those *busslin* she loves so much, and you can spend some time with her...with us." His lips formed a tiny, hopeful smile that looked like it could be scared away by a single stern look.

"*Jah*, I'd be glad to stop by," Grace answered eagerly, already looking forward to spending more time with Aaron and his adorable little sister. Yet she was unable to shake her suspicion that the man who sat beside her had something more important on his mind than a friendly visit.

Grace settled against the buggy seat and savored the respite from the storm cloud that had oppressed her for the past several months. Aaron was slowly coming out of his shell, and she didn't want to scare him back into it by being nosy. She reluctantly reminded herself that if Aaron did indeed have something significant to say, he would say it when he was ready.

"You're gonna wear a hole in those floorboards if you don't quit pacing."

"*Ach*, sorry, *Mamm*." Aaron scooted across the front porch and lowered himself onto the bench swing. Keeping his eyes on the quiet lane in the distance, he slowly rocked the swing, hoping that the gentle, repetitive motion would help him to settle down.

His mother, Becky, wore a knowing smile as she sat on the top porch step, shelling fresh-picked peas into a large metal bowl. "I don't know who's more excited for Grace to arrive, you or that *dochder* of mine."

Aaron chose not to reply, not wanting to fuel his mother's growing speculation. She didn't need to know that her son had been unable to stop thinking about Grace since he'd arrived home from yesterday's work frolic, though he was sure that his sudden upbeat attitude had already revealed that. The more he thought about it, Grace seemed to be the only person he felt truly comfortable around, except for Annie, of course.

He drummed his fingers on the armrest of the porch swing, keeping his gaze fixed on the lane as he waited for Grace's arrival. His eyes started to burn and he wondered if he'd forgotten to blink.

After what felt like centuries, Aaron finally spotted a slender Amish woman walking briskly down the lane. He felt his chest tighten as the woman drew nearer, and when he recognized Grace's raven-colored hair and lovely face, he leaped up from his seat so quickly that it swung back and banged against the white paneling of the house. "Grace!" he hollered, then waved broadly to catch her attention.

Becky flinched and dropped the pea pod she'd just picked up. "Best not to shout on the Lord's Day, *sohn*."

Aaron shamefully apologized to his mother and did his best to stand in place as Grace jogged toward the house, the skirt of her navy-blue dress flapping around her shins as she ran. Wasting no time, Aaron bounded down the porch stairs to meet Grace on the front lawn.

"Hello," he said quietly, doing his best to contain his excitement. "*Wie ghets?*"

"I'm doing *gut*," Grace responded with a smile. She sounded slightly winded and took a deep breath. "I've been looking forward to seeing those *busslin* that you told me about." She peered around Aaron and grinned at his mother. "*Denki* for having me over."

Becky waved her hand through the air. "*Ach*, you're *wilkumme* to visit us anytime you'd like, Grace. It's nice to see you outside of church." She continued shelling peas without needing to look at her hands. Each of the peas made a melodic ping as they dropped into the bowl that rested on her knees. "We've all been *very* anxious to see you this afternoon."

"*Mamm*, please," Aaron begged as he turned to give his mother a pleading look. She made him sound like a lovestruck schoolboy. He rubbed circles into his temples with his fingertips, hoping he wouldn't pass out from the embarrassment.

"Have you invited your guest to stay for supper?" Then Becky turned her attention to Grace. "We're having roast beef tonight, and there'll be more than enough to go around."

Grace licked her lips. "That sounds *appenditlich*. I made some chicken pot pies before I went to bed last night, and told my *daadi* to reheat one of those if I wasn't home by six o'clock, so I can definitely stay for the meal."

When his mother issued a playful wink at him, Aaron pretended not to see it and hoped that Grace had missed the teasing gesture. "L-let's go find Annie. I'm sure she's eager to see you." Without waiting for Grace, he turned on his heels and hurried away.

"What was that about?" Grace asked as she dashed to catch up with Aaron, soon matching his long stride.

Aaron was so flustered by his mother's not-so-subtle ribbing that his feet almost became tangled. Unable to even glance over at Grace, Aaron stared straight ahead at his father's gigantic white barn as he slowed his pace. "*Vell*, I've never had a female friend before. *Mamm* probably assumed that we're courting."

"*Ach*, you look so worried," Grace groaned playfully as she gave him a little shove. "Would it be so awful if someone thought that I was your *aldi*?"

Aaron stumbled, caught his balance then snickered at her good-natured question. It was hard for him to keep a straight face around Grace. "It's not awful, but it would probably be shocking to folks who know me. I never had any luck with courting."

"Oh?"

Aaron kicked at a dandelion in the grass, sending its puffy seeds floating off in all directions. "I briefly pursued a few different *maedels* in my late teens, once I started attending functions for *die youngie*. It took me lots of time to build up the courage to ask if I could give them a ride home in my courting buggy, but every one of them turned me down. It seemed like a waste of time to gather all of that courage only to be rejected, so I stopped making an effort."

"*Vell*, all those women missed out on a *wunderbaar* man, that's for certain sure." She glanced up at him as she offered a sincere grin. "I know the right woman for you is out there, Aaron. You're too caring and kind to be a bachelor forever."

Aaron started to respond but one look at Grace's dazzling eyes and the cute way that she smiled up at him took his breath away. He faked a cough in hopes that she wouldn't notice his flustered state, and in doing so, he inhaled one of the dandelion seeds that were floating past. He choked and sputtered before finally spitting the fuzzy seed out.

Having witnessed the ordeal, Grace burst out in peals of laughter and was barely able to catch her breath as she wiped tears from her eyes.

Aaron couldn't help but give in to his own fit of chuckles. If anyone else had caught him in such a state, he'd have assumed they were laughing at him. Yet Grace had a way of putting him at ease, and thankfully he also found some humor in the embarrassing moment. It was just one more thing that endeared him to her, and he was reminded again of his growing desire to court Grace. He wasn't ready to make his move just yet, but if things continued to go so well between them, he could be putting his heart on the line sooner than later.

The friends entered the barn through the milk house, where a large gas-powered refrigerated milk tank and milking equipment were housed, then rounded the corner and passed by the cattle stalls, all of which were empty and waiting for the Holsteins to return from their day spent grazing in the pasture. The simple tune of a child's humming could be heard as they approached the end of the barn where the horse stalls were located, causing both of them to grin.

Aaron opened the door to the vacant stall, and sure enough, Annie was curled up in the far corner with all five kittens in her lap. The gray mother cat sat beside the young girl, grooming her sleek fur.

"Look who's here," Aaron beamed as he and Grace entered the stall.

Annie looked up and her face brightened as if it was the first day of summer vacation. "Grace!" Her exclamation startled the kittens awake, except for the one that had been kneading against the raggedy old blanket that covered her lap. "You came to see me!"

"*Jah*, and I wanted to meet these *busslin* I've been hearing so much about." Grace grinned as she lowered herself into the straw beside Annie. "May I hold one of them?"

"You can each hold one." Annie beamed. She gently handed Grace the black-and-white kitten. When Aaron was seated on her other side, Annie handed him the orange kitten, who seemed to be the most rambunctious of the litter.

"Have any of these *busslin* got a name?" Grace asked, giggling at the black-and-white kitten as it batted at the ribbons of her *kapp*.

Annie stroked the mother cat's head as a hint of sadness crept onto her face. "*Daed* said we have to find all of the *busslin* homes, and I don't think it's fair for me to name them if they are going to new *familye*." Her brown eyes suddenly brightened. "Would you like a *bussli*, Grace? I know you'd take real *gut* care of it."

"My *daadi* has been having trouble getting around lately and a playful *bussli* might get underfoot," Grace answered, letting the child down gently.

"Playful is one way to describe them," Aaron added as the kitten he held squirmed out of his grasp, climbed up to his shoulder, then jumped onto his head, its little legs shaking as it tried to keep its balance.

"Maybe he thinks he needs to keep your head warm," Annie chortled, her girlish giggles causing both adults to smile.

Aaron helped the kitten down from his head and set it next to its mother. He listened as Annie told Grace about each one of the kittens. Grace seemed taken with Annie's commentary, often asking the young girl questions and complimenting her excellent care of the baby cats. Aaron couldn't help but notice the nurturing way that Grace spoke and the way that Annie seemed to be enthralled with Grace's presence. Not only was Grace warm and caring, but she was as lovely as a summer sunrise, and Aaron concluded that her old beau must have been out of his mind if he jilted such a treasure of a woman.

"Hello? Anyone in here?" A familiar male voice echoed through the barn and interrupted Aaron's thoughts and Grace and Annie's conversation.

Annie let out a gasp. She quickly placed the remaining kittens next to their mother, scrambled to her feet, and then darted out of the horse stall. "Noah's here!"

Aaron held in a sigh as he stood, shook the straw from his trousers, then helped Grace to her feet. Before he

could tell Grace what was going on, Noah came saunter-
ing around the corner wearing his signature dashing smile.
Annie followed close behind him, nearly tickled pink by
Noah's surprise arrival.

"Looks like I'm not the only one here to see the *busslin*
that Annie's been talking about," Noah said as he split a
look between Aaron and Grace. "I'm Noah King," he said
as he extended his hand to Grace.

"Noah's our oldest *bruder*," Annie said, throwing her
arms around Noah and giving him a bear hug. "He lives
over in Smoketown."

"I'm Grace Ebersol," Grace said as she accepted Noah's
hand and gave it a light shake. "I'm Eli Ebersol's *enkelin*,
and a friend of Aaron's."

Noah's eyebrows—which almost appeared to have been
manicured—rose in surprise. "Really? *Vell*, it's a pleasure
to meet you." He released Grace's hand and then issued
his brother a playfully suspicious smirk.

Aaron cringed with embarrassment. He stared up at the
barn's rafters, noticing a few cobwebs swaying in the slight
cross breeze. Ever since Noah had married and moved to
the neighboring community of Smoketown, he'd seen less
and less of his seemingly flawless sibling, and that was
just fine with him.

Aaron's gaze dropped to the cement floor, and he felt a
minor pang of guilt. Noah wasn't a bad person and didn't
deserve to be thought of with contempt. Sure, they hadn't
exactly gotten along as children, especially when Noah
had teased him for being overly shy and outshined him in
all ways possible, but they were both adults now. There
was no need for any sort of competition, especially since
Noah would always win.

"Did ya really come to see my *busslin*?" Annie asked as she tugged on Noah's hand.

Noah chuckled at Annie's enthusiasm. "I do want to see those kittens of yours, but I'm actually here for supper." He turned his attention to the adults. "My *fraa* is visiting a sick *freind*, so I was hoping that I could share the evening meal here."

"*Mamm* said she's fixed plenty to eat, so I'm sure that won't be a problem," Aaron replied softly, though secretly he wanted to jump for joy. If Noah was going to stick around for supper, there was a very strong possibility that the dinner conversation would revolve around Noah, which would take the focus off of him and Grace. He had always felt that his parents favored their eldest child, and with Noah being so outgoing and talkative, Aaron could effortlessly fade into the background. If all the attention was focused on Noah, it would be less likely that someone would make a comment about him and Grace courting, which might scare her away, and that would never do.

Everything will be fine as long as Noah takes his usual place in the spotlight, Aaron thought as the four of them exited the barn and headed for the house. Perhaps his brother's unexpected arrival was a blessing in disguise, as long as it meant that there would be no more talk of him and Grace courting.

Chapter Nine

As Annie led her through the back door of the two-story farmhouse, Grace immediately noticed how neat and clean the home was. They crossed through the tidy mudroom and then entered the well-lit kitchen where they were immediately greeted with the delicious scents of a home-cooked meal. Aaron's mother had several steaming dishes lined up along the counter, each one of the piping-hot plates wafting mouth-watering aromas in to air.

Grace closed her eyes and inhaled deeply. "It all smells so *gut*, Mrs. King. What can I help you with?"

The middle-aged, stout woman glanced up from the mashed potatoes that she was scooping into a large serving bowl. "Call me Becky, dear. You're our guest, so all you need to do is take a seat."

"Sit next to me," Annie begged, grinning up at Grace and tugging on her hand.

"I was hoping you'd ask," Grace replied, winking at the sweet girl. She followed Annie to the long oak table and had to hold back a giggle when Annie pulled out a chair for her. She graciously thanked Aaron's sister for her hospitality while wishing that she had a younger sibling of her own.

Annie beamed adoringly at Grace as she lowered herself onto the adjacent chair. She started asking her about her favorite foods, but before Grace could answer Annie let out a gasp. "*Mamm*, we need to set an extra place."

"I already set an extra place for Grace," Becky answered, gesturing to the place setting in front of Grace after she set a steaming bowl of peas and a bowl of mashed potatoes in the center of the table.

"*Nee*, Noah's here too. He said Hannah went to visit a friend, so he came to have supper with us," Annie explained as she jumped up from her seat. She dashed to the cupboard and retrieved another plate.

Becky's face lit up and she smiled broadly. "How nice! It will be *gut* to see that eldest *bu* of mine." She rushed back to the counter to bring the rest of the food to the table. "Is he still outside?"

"*Jah*." Annie bobbed her head enthusiastically as she squeezed another plate and some silverware between the other table settings. "I told him that *Daed* was reading the paper on the front porch, so he and Aaron went over there."

"*Vell*, this food won't get any warmer. Please go tell them that it's time to eat. Your two other *brieder* are taking naps, so you better wake them before they miss supper."

Annie obediently darted out of the room.

Grace remained seated and made polite small talk with Aaron's *mamm* as she retrieved a large plastic pitcher from the refrigerator and circled the table, filling each glass with cold water. Though she'd met Aaron's parents and younger siblings at recent church services, and her brief introduction to Noah had been pleasant, it was hard to ignore the flutter she felt in her chest. Surely it wasn't nervousness. What did she have to be nervous about? It wasn't like she and Aaron were a courting couple and she needed to make a good impression on his family.

The sound of heavy work boots clomping across the linoleum floor drew her attention. She looked up to see Steve, Aaron's tall, bearded father, enter the room. He was followed by Noah, who had his father's masculine looks but his mother's ruddy hair.

Then came Abe and Sam, Aaron's two younger brothers, both in their mid-teens and the only two members of the family who had blue eyes. Both boys were sleepy-eyed but seemed to come alive when they saw all the food their mother had prepared.

Then Annie scampered into the kitchen and resumed her spot at the table next to Grace.

Finally, Aaron slunk into the room behind his family members. With his head down he scurried to the table as if trying to remain unnoticed.

Grace was pleased when Aaron took a seat at the table directly across from her. She noticed his downcast gaze and tight-lipped grimace and wondered what had brought on his change in disposition. He seemed to be enjoying himself earlier that afternoon and suddenly it was as if he'd been covered by a heavy storm cloud. Had she done or said something to upset him?

"Aaron," she started quietly, hoping not to draw too much attention. "Are you—"

"You're Eli Ebersol's *enkelin*, ain't ya?" This came from Abe as he took a seat beside Aaron.

"It's Grace, right?" Sam asked as he sat on Aaron's other side, then loudly scooted his chair closer to the table.

"*Jah*, that's me." Grace offered a polite grin, though she wished Aaron's younger brothers hadn't interrupted her. Something was clearly off with Aaron, and it would bother her until she knew what it was. She found it odd that Aaron's brothers hadn't said anything about his sudden change of mood, but perhaps they were just too ravenous to notice.

She glanced across the room where both Steve and Becky were chatting with Noah and making over him as if he were a celebrity. Steve gazed at his oldest boy proudly and gave Noah several pats on the shoulder. Becky wrapped both of her hands around one of Noah's, smiling up at him and hanging on his every word.

Grace watched the scene with narrowed eyes and felt even more confused. The way that Mr. and Mrs. King were fawning over Noah was peculiar. Perhaps he didn't visit often and his parents were just glad to see him. But that didn't make sense. Annie had mentioned that Noah and his wife lived in Smoketown, which was only a brief buggy ride from Bird-in-Hand. Surely a son who lived so close to his parents would visit often.

"When are we gonna eat?" Annie's question interrupted Grace's ponderings. "My belly's roarin' like a lion."

Everyone except Aaron chuckled.

Noah seated himself beside Annie as Steve and Becky took their places at the head and foot of the table.

Steve bowed his head for the silent prayer, but it bounced back up when he did a double-take. "Hello, Grace. I didn't know you were here."

"Aaron invited me to see Annie's *busslin*, and your *fraa* invited me to stay for the meal." She glanced down at her plate, hoping that her presence wasn't an intrusion now that Noah had arrived.

Steve's thick eyebrows shot up. "Is that so?" He glanced over at Aaron while wearing a poorly controlled smirk.

Saying nothing, Aaron's face was soon the shade of the cherry tomatoes that were a part of Becky's salad.

"We're glad to have you with us," Becky added, perhaps sensing Aaron's mortification.

"And we're happy to have our eldest *sohn* here as well," Steve said as he made a brief gesture toward Noah. "Have you two had a chance to meet?"

"We did," Noah answered, leaning forward to see around Annie.

Grace nodded with a small smile, but her eyes soon wandered back over to Aaron, who still hadn't said a word or looked up from his folded hands that he'd placed on the table.

"Now that we're all acquainted, let's give thanks to *Gott* and then fill our bellies," Steve said. He bowed his head and everyone else did the same.

After the silent prayer was over, the serving platters started being passed around the table nearly as quickly as the conversation had resumed.

"Grace, did anyone tell you that Noah is the bishop of the Smoketown church district?" Steve asked as he forked two slices of roast beef onto his plate. "At twenty-seven, he's the youngest man to be elected bishop that I know of."

Grace spooned some mashed potatoes on her plate and then held the bowl for Annie as she did the same. "*Nee*, I didn't know." When Annie placed the spoon back in the bowl, Grace passed the bowl to Becky. She was impressed by Noah's high-ranking position in the church, and it was plain to see that his parents were proud of their son's standing. "The community must admire you, *jah*?"

Noah smiled graciously before taking a sip of his water. "Being the leader of the flock is both a blessing and something that I am humbled by. I'm just glad that I have my whole life ahead of me to serve *Gott* and the People."

"Guess what happened when we were playing with the *busslin*," Annie said with a mouthful of buttered noodles. "One of the *busslin* got away from Aaron and climbed up onto his head."

A light chuckle came from each person seated at the table.

"Those kittens are growing up fast and are ready to start exploring the world," Aaron quietly added, subtly winking at his kid sister.

"They sure are," Steve grinned. He poured a small amount of homemade dressing onto his salad. "So, Noah, I heard through the grapevine that you were recently spotted at the New Holland Auction. Did you get yourself a new horse?"

Noah took a roll from the bread basket. "I bought a six-year-old gelding, and I'm going to pick him up tomorrow."

"What kind of horse is it?" Aaron asked, barely above a whisper.

"Did you get a *gut* deal on him?" their father questioned at the same time, the volume of his voice dwarfing Aaron's.

Noah nodded as he sliced into the dinner roll and slathered it with butter. "*Jah*, I spent only three-quarters of what I was prepared to spend, so I'd say that was a bargain."

The corners of Grace's mouth drooped when she realized that Noah had ignored his brother's question. She didn't want to jump to conclusions. Maybe Noah just hadn't heard Aaron over their *daed*. Turning her attention to Aaron, she could see a hint of disappointment in his eyes. When he noticed her gaze on him, he gave a half-hearted smile and a little shrug. Wasn't he going to make another attempt to try to be a part of his family's conversation?

"Aaron, did you tell your *familye* your news about the woodshop?" Grace asked, hoping to draw her friend into the conversation.

Aaron opened his mouth but before he could utter a single word, Abe spoke up. "*Jah*, our *bruder* is going to be a business owner."

"It's an exciting time for Aaron," Becky said as she reached over and gave her son's hand a few pats. "Noah has big things on the horizon too. His *fraa* is in a family way."

"*Jah*, we'll have our first *kinnskind* come December," Steve added, his voice sounding as jolly as a Christmas card. "Have you and your *fraa* discussed any names for the *boppli*, Noah?"

Grace fought to control her expression, though it was a difficult task. It sure seemed like Aaron's family had glossed over his success only to shine the spotlight back on Noah. Maybe they were simply overexcited by Noah's visit, but the dour look on Aaron's face led her to believe that this type of interaction was a regular occurrence.

Filled with pity, she watched her friend as he stared down, pushing his food around his plate with his fork. It struck Grace that Aaron's low self-confidence and meek ways might be a product of living in the shadow of his seemingly perfect older brother.

What a shame, Grace thought as she glanced down at her overflowing plate, suddenly having little appetite. She imagined how she would feel if she were in his position, and concluded that what he needed most was someone who would listen to him, who *wanted* to listen to him.

She'd make sure to remind him that he could always talk to her. Hopefully he'd open up.

Grace insisted on helping "redd up" after the meal was over, and Aaron quietly enjoyed watching the friendly back-and-forth between her and his mother and Annie. *Mamm* insisted that a guest shouldn't lift a finger, and Grace persisted that she wanted to pitch in as if it were her greatest desire. *Mamm* eventually caved and allowed Grace to dry the dishes after they'd been washed.

Daed and Aaron's younger brothers seemed anxious to continue their conversation with Noah, and the four of them headed outside to enjoy the cool evening air and chew the fat. Though Aaron assumed that Annie would run outside to play or try to goad Noah into holding the kittens, he was pleasantly surprised when Annie offered to put away the dishes after Grace had dried them.

Unsure of whether he should follow after the menfolk or stay with the women, so as to not abandon Grace, Aaron felt out of place in his own home. He remained seated at the table and enjoyed listening to their conversation.

She fits in perfectly, Aaron thought as he smiled to himself, *like a missing puzzle piece.*

After some more visiting and one last look at Annie's kittens, Grace announced that it was time for her to return to her grandfather's cottage. Aaron offered to walk her home since dusk had fallen. The sleepy countryside was a safe place, and certainly no harm would befall her if she walked home alone, but he wasn't ready to part ways with Grace just yet.

Instead of walking along the road, Aaron and Grace cut through his father's property and neighboring farmland, squeezing together on the narrow dirt paths so they wouldn't step on any of the growing crops. Though the sun had set, nightfall hadn't fully settled in. The ever-darkening lavender sky above nicely complemented the lush green surroundings. Cornstalks whispered against each other in the gentle breeze, and lightning bugs twinkled above fields of soybeans, wheat, and alfalfa.

Aaron silently strolled beside Grace, carrying a large flashlight in one hand for the trip back to his house. He relished inhaling the clean country air, sweet with the scent of fresh-cut hay, and he found comfort in Grace's gentle humming. The melody coming from her was a familiar church hymn, and he was deeply content just to listen and be near her.

"I enjoyed having supper with you and your *familye*," Grace suddenly stated, swinging her arms to match her stride, "but I'm wondering if you enjoyed it as well."

Aaron's serene grin twisted in confusion. "Of course, I did. *Mamm* is a real *gut* cook."

Grace tittered, her laugh nearly identical to a robin's chirp. "That's not what I'm asking," she said as she gave him a lighthearted shove. Seconds later, her beautiful smile fizzled out, and her lips formed a straight line. She glanced over at him with concern written across her face, like the bold print of a newspaper's front-page headline. "I noticed that you seemed to get quiet when Noah showed up."

Aaron wasn't sure what to say, but he was certain

that he didn't want to discuss his feelings about his older brother.

Grace held up her palms in defense. "At first I thought that maybe I'd said or done something that bothered you, but as we ate, I realized that probably wasn't the case." She stopped walking and grabbed Aaron's hand, halting him as well. "Is everything *oll recht* between you and Noah?"

"*Jah*," Aaron answered, unable to look Grace in the eye. He stared past her into the sea of cornstalks, wishing he could disappear into them. "Noah just has more to say than I do."

Grace dropped his hand, staring at him with a mixture of suspicion and sympathy.

Aaron sighed deeply. He took off his straw hat and ran his fingers through his hair. "It seems like… I mean, sometimes it feels… I don't know how to say—"

"Say what's on your heart," Grace interrupted, gazing up at him tenderly. "I'll listen, and I won't judge."

Aaron placed his hat back on his head and started forward. If it was anyone but Grace walking beside him, he'd think more than twice about saying what he was about to share. "I think my parents have a habit of favoring Noah. It's unintentional, I'm sure of it. They're the best *mamm* and *daed* that I could ask for."

He stared straight ahead, taking in the purplish sky yet not comforted by its beauty. He waited for Grace to assure him that he'd misinterpreted the situation, but when she said nothing but dashed to catch up with him, he continued.

"Maybe it's because Noah was their firstborn, or maybe it's because he's more outgoing than I am. It's easy to hide in the background when everyone focuses on him, which probably didn't help my tendencies to be shy."

They paused as two brown rabbits darted out of the cornstalks, crossed the narrow dirt path, and disappeared into the soybeans. The tall, leafy plants rustled as the bunnies scurried around them.

"Noah teased me an awful lot about my shyness when we were *kinner*," Aaron went on. "As we got older and became of courting age, he insinuated that no *maedels* would be interested in me and that I would always be a failure."

Grace uttered a quiet gasp.

"There'll be none of that," Aaron stopped her, forcing a smile. "Really, I have no hard feelings toward anyone in my *familye*, parents and Noah included. Noah and I are both adults now, and we get along just fine. Strangely, I even look up to him because he's everything I'm not."

Grace shot him another uncertain glance.

"Seriously, I'm fine. It's just the way things have always been."

Grace nodded, seemingly accepting the explanation for his meek ways.

They continued ambling through the picturesque, rolling farmland, neither one of them saying anything. Crickets hiding in the hayfield they were passing chipped their nightly serenade, magnifying the silence between them.

Though the night air was light and cool, Aaron felt his forehead starting to perspire. *What is she thinking,* he wondered, hoping that he hadn't shocked Grace with his candidness.

"I understand why you feel the way that you do and why you're quiet sometimes," Grace suddenly said, much to Aaron's relief. They neared the crest of the hill they'd been ascending when Grace spoke again. "I hope you feel free to say whatever you want around me."

"*Ach*, I do," Aaron sincerely replied, though he chose not to let Grace know that she was the only person who made him feel that way. Though it was getting darker by the minute, Aaron could make out the Ebersol cottage at the bottom of the other side of the hill. Once again, he found himself dreading parting ways with his kindhearted, blue-eyed friend. "You've become a very special person to me in a short time, and I know I can trust you."

Grace beamed at him, her eyes sparkling in the moonlight. She took a step closer to him then quickly stepped back and whispered, "There's *daadi*'s *haus*," gesturing toward the cottage. "*Gut nacht*."

Before Aaron could reply, Grace scurried away and flitted toward the small stone cottage. He waited until she tiptoed up to the door and slipped noiselessly inside before he turned and headed for home.

His mind rushed with ideas as he flicked on the flashlight, its narrow, bright beam guiding him through the maze of dense greenery. Grace had responded to his most private emotions with grace, just as her name suggested. The intimate conversation had certainly strengthened their bond, yet she seemed to startle when Aaron gave her a glimpse of his growing feelings for her.

As if on cue, nagging self-doubt attacked him once again, like a monster stalking his every move from deep within the cornstalks. He had a great thing going with Grace, and asking if he could court her risked ruining that. He began to second-guess his decision to pursue her.

Maybe he should wait to make his move until he was sure she was interested in him. He couldn't jeopardize their friendship for anything less.

Chapter Ten

The following Sunday was a church Sunday for the Bird-in-Hand church district, and much to Aaron's chagrin, the biweekly service was scheduled to be held at his family's farm. Normally Aaron didn't mind the twice-yearly duty of hosting and all the responsibilities that came with it. However, all of the extra work and preparations meant that he had precious little time to spend with Grace, and for sorting out his emotions.

Aaron asked Eli if he could work half days that week so he could hurry home and assist with the preparations for hosting church. Eli agreed without hesitation, having hosted their district's church services dozens of times throughout his life, and understanding all that went into preparing a temporary house of worship. So promptly at noon each day, Aaron hurried his horse home where *Mamm* or *Daed* always had some project waiting for him. His parents weren't prideful people, yet they took great care in cleaning every nook and cranny of their house and barn.

"Why do we gotta clean our bedrooms too?" Annie asked before evening prayer one night. "Nobody's gonna look for dust bunnies or even go upstairs on Sunday."

"Our friends and neighbors might not look into every

room, but *Gott* can see all, and it's best to have a tidy place to worship on the Lord's Day," *Mamm* responded with deep conviction.

So, it was settled. The entire King family worked together, making sure that absolutely everything was in order. Every inch of the floor was scrubbed clean. The window panes were washed, both inside and out, and were so clean that it nearly appeared as if they weren't there. Gas lamps were filled with oil, should the coming Sunday turn out to be cloudy. Every area rug was taken outdoors, beaten, then left to air out. Each piece of furniture was dusted and polished. The lawn was mown and the flower beds were weeded. Even the barn was cleaned spic and span, with Annie joking that Aaron knocked down the cobwebs before the spiders even had a chance to spin them.

On Saturday morning, the removable partitions that separated the kitchen and the living room were taken away to create one enormous space. The bench wagon arrived shortly after, and Aaron and his younger brothers made quick work of assembling the backless wooden benches while *Daed* arranged them in neat rows, half on one side of the huge open space and half on the other.

After an exhausting week, Aaron should have been glad for the three-hour service, a time in which he would sit instead of scurrying around and find comfort in God's word. Instead, he felt stressed and deeply uncomfortable. With so many bodies in the house on a late August morning, it had become incredibly stuffy. The mugginess, though, wasn't the true reason for his discomfort.

What am I going to do about Grace? he silently pondered, tuning out Bishop Lapp's singsong sermon. His interest in her grew with each day that passed, yet his relentless self-doubt remained steady. Every day, just like clockwork, he'd work up the courage to ask her out, then change his mind a few hours later. Asking Grace if he could court her presented so many risks. If he declared his interest in her and she didn't share the same feelings, their friendship might be ruined. She might think him inconsiderate for proposing courtship after she'd so plainly stated her stance against it.

And if I upset Grace, Eli might think twice about passing his business along to me, Aaron considered, stricken with crippling worry. What was worth more to him, the chance to own his own business, or the opportunity to woo the woman of his dreams?

He scanned the women's side of the large room in search of Grace's lovely face as he pondered all of the things that could go wrong if he were to make his interest in her known.

But isn't risking all of that worth a chance at winning Grace's heart? Aaron knew that he'd never forgive himself if he passed up the opportunity to develop their friendship into something much more. *I'm done hemming and hawing. The next time I run into Grace, I'm going to ask if I may court her.*

Determined yet terrified, Aaron visually scoured the women's side of the room once more, having not located Grace during his first search. After not being able to find her a second time, he wondered if maybe she was seated in the back row, or perhaps she was obstructed from his line of sight by the many similarly dressed women.

When the service was over and the light meal of soup and sandwiches had been served, Aaron had still not been able to locate Grace. Concerned, he sought out Eli, who was chatting with some other elderly men, their beards all similarly long and gray.

Aaron stepped up to the tight cluster and was about to clear his throat, too timid to simply announce his presence with a proper greeting, when Eli turned and smiled at him.

"*Guder mariye*, *yung* Mister King," Eli greeted him with a particularly peaceful grin. "*Wie bischt*?"

"F-fine," Aaron replied, flashing what he hoped wasn't an awkward smile to the group of church elders. "I was just wondering where Grace is. I can't seem to find her."

"She stayed home today," Eli answered, his pleasant expression fading a bit. "Came down with a terrible headache last night. This morning, when she didn't have breakfast ready, I went to see if she was *oll recht* and found her still asleep in bed." He leaned on his cane as his shoulders rose in an unsteady shrug. "Thought it best to let her rest, and I slipped out of the *haus* as quietly as I could."

Aaron frowned. "I'm sorry to hear that. Does she need anything? What can I do to help?"

"*Nee*, I'm sure it will pass and she'll soon be as *gut* as new, but there is something that I'd like to discuss with you." Eli turned back toward the group of men he'd been talking to before Aaron's arrival, nodded at each one of them, and bid a quick farewell before suggesting that he and Aaron head outdoors to talk.

Aaron agreed and followed Eli out of the much-too-warm house, eager to get some fresh air. He was keen to hear what was on his employer's mind.

Once they were seated side by side on the porch swing, Eli got right to the point. "I wanted to say *denki* for being such a *gut* friend to my Gracie. She's been more cheerful since you two started getting close, and that hasn't gone unnoticed."

"No thanks needed," Aaron replied sincerely as he pushed his feet against the porch to get the swing moving. "I have to admit that I was *naerfich* to approach her, but I'm thankful that you encouraged me to do so." He stared straight ahead, his eyes drifting to the cluster of wildflowers that grew across the lane. "She's quickly become my truest friend."

Eli wore a wrinkled grin that stretched from ear to ear. "Is it safe to assume that you two are a pair?"

Though he could feel Eli's gaze fixed on him, Aaron didn't take his eyes off the wildflowers, lest Eli be able to see into the depths of his soul. Just how much was he willing to share with Grace's grandfather? Yet if he didn't confide in Eli, and glean some of his advice, he wouldn't have anyone else to discuss matters of the heart with.

"I'm…uh… I'm planning on asking Grace if I may come calling, but I'm worried that will upset her, or that she might turn me down like all the other *maedels* that I've tried to court." He felt his palms grow moist with perspiration and dried them on his black trousers. "These things never seem to work out for me, so I'm hesitant to be hopeful."

Eli worked his mouth, mulling over Aaron's concern. "Do you love *Gott*, our Heavenly Father, Aaron?"

"Of course, I do." Aaron's head turned to face Eli so quickly that he pulled a muscle in his neck. "What does that have to do with courting Grace?" Aaron asked as he rubbed the sore spot on his neck.

"The book of Romans, chapter eight, verse twenty-eight says 'And we know that all things work together for good to them that love God, to them who are called according to His purpose.'" He paused, watching as a group of children buzzed through the yard like a swarm of honeybees. "So, it seems to me," he slowly continued, "that if you have a love for *Gott*, you have nothing to worry about, ain't so?"

"*Jah*, but people still have free will," Aaron countered, finding it difficult to accept that the answer to his dilemma was that simple. "*Gott* won't force Grace to take an interest in me just because I've developed one for her."

"That's true," Eli admitted. He raised his right hand, extended his knobby pointer finger, and tapped the side of his head. "But something tells me that won't be a problem."

Aaron said nothing but continued to rock the swing, hoping with every ounce of his soul that Eli's instincts were correct.

The next day, Grace awoke to the sound of raindrops pelting against the nearby window. She stretched and groaned, then let out a sigh of relief when she realized the agonizing headache that she'd recently suffered had disappeared during the night. Perhaps it was the white willow bark capsules that *Daadi* had insisted she take after supper last night, or it could have been the unusual amount of bedrest that had cured her ailment. Whatever the reason for her recovery, Grace was extremely thankful.

"*Denki*, Lord," she said out loud before pushing aside the light summer quilt and dressing for the day. Though she was feeling much better, she still took great care when brushing her hair, parting it down the middle, rolling it on the sides, and fashioning it into a low bun, lest she be too rough and invite the headache to return.

As she pinned her *kapp* into place, she glanced at the

battery-powered alarm clock on the nightstand, then did a double take. It was nearly noon! She was typically an early riser and despised wasted daylight, even when the sun was covered by heavy rain clouds.

She rushed out of the room, zoomed down the short hall, and screeched to a halt when she saw Eli making a sandwich at the kitchen counter.

"*Daadi*, I'm so sorry I wasn't up sooner," she apologized breathlessly, realizing that her grandfather had started his day without a decent breakfast. "Let me finish making that sandwich for you."

Eli waved Grace away. "After my *fraa* passed away, I became an expert *saendwitsch*-maker. You sit yourself down and I'll make lunch for both of us."

"Really, *Daadi*," Grace protested, riddled with guilt, "I don't—"

"You were never one to disobey your elders," Eli interrupted her, looking over his shoulder with a smirk. "I'm surprised you're starting to do so now."

Grace giggled and shook her head. "Have it your way," she said with a playful wink. She moved to the cupboard, grabbed two plastic tumblers, then went to the refrigerator. "Should we have meadow tea or lemonade?"

"Lemonade sounds *gut*," Eli said as he spread leftover egg salad across slices of homemade wheat bread.

Grace opened the refrigerator and reached for the pitcher of lemonade. "I'm embarrassed that I lazed around so much yesterday and this morning," she admitted as she filled each glass with the chilled beverage. "I'm sorry I wasn't up to fixing your breakfast."

"I'm not," Eli replied as he plated both sandwiches and

then shuffled to the table. "If your body needs rest, rest is what you should give it. Are you feeling better today?"

"*Ach*, very much so." Grace placed the pitcher back in the refrigerator. She picked up both cups and then turned to join her grandfather at the table but froze in place when her eyes landed on a lovely sight.

A breathtaking bouquet of wildflowers sat in a mason jar in the middle of the table. The striking wildflower arrangement, including daisies, cosmos, baby's breath, and some greenery, hadn't been there yesterday. The bouquet brought a nice dash of the Lord's colorful creation into the plain room.

"When did you pick these?" Grace asked as she took a seat at the table across from *Daadi*, unable to take her eyes off the colorful bundle of flowers.

"I didn't. Yesterday at church Aaron was asking 'bout you, and when I told him you were under the weather, he seemed awful concerned. He showed up for work today with these flowers in hand, and said he'd picked them this morning to cheer you up." Eli glanced at the flowers and then at Grace, his bright smile making him appear nearly a decade younger. "I think Aaron likes you, Gracie."

Before Grace could react, Eli bowed his head for the silent prayer. Grace mimicked him, though she was completely unable to focus on expressing her thanks to the Lord. The fact that Aaron had gone out of his way to handpick and deliver a bouquet of wildflowers for her certainly put weight behind *Daadi*'s suspicion.

Maybe the flowers were just an expression of friendship. *Daadi* could be looking too much into Aaron's gesture. She considered all of the possibilities with her head still bowed when she should have been thanking the Lord for her meal. Yet she and Aaron had grown fond of each other and she found comfort in his quiet, unassuming ways. *Is it possible that he is interested in me, and I am also interested in him?*

Raising her head before Eli did, she reached for her cup with a shaky hand and took a long drink. She had to be honest with herself; she was attracted to Aaron. He was good-looking, with his wavy, golden-brown hair, dark eyes, and tall, muscular frame. Yet there was so much more that drew Grace to Aaron, beyond his handsome, masculine appearance. He was gentle in both manner and tone. He cared deeply for others, and he was a great listener. True, he had his flaws, but he was humble, patient, hardworking, and kind, which was more than enough to catch the eye of any single Amish woman.

The screen door squeaked open, and in came Aaron with a small blue cooler in hand. His eyes brightened when he noticed Grace at the table. "*Wie ghets*? Are you feeling any better?"

"I am, *denki* for asking." She heard the unsteadiness in her voice, hoping that no one else had noticed. "*Denki* also for the flowers. They're just lovely!"

Aaron gave a closed-mouthed smile, nodded, and took a seat at the table.

"Can I fix you something for lunch?" Grace asked as she rose from her chair. "We're having egg salad sandwiches."

"*Nee*, I brought lunch from home today," Aaron answered as he placed the petite cooler on the table in front of him. "I didn't expect you to make anything since you were feeling poorly yesterday." He bowed his head in silent prayer, then opened the cooler, and took out a slice of shoofly pie, an apple, and several pieces of baked chicken.

When he dug into the pie first, Grace held back a chuckle. She lowered herself back onto her seat, unable to deny her affection for the quirky fellow seated beside her.

Seconds later, her grin melted into a frown. If she gave her heart to Aaron, there was a chance that she could be emotionally devastated again. Who was to say that everything would work out if they started courting?

Was she willing to risk breaking her heart for a second time? Could a person survive such emotional turmoil twice? She stared down at her half-eaten sandwich. Looking up, her eyes darted between the bouquet in the center of the table and Aaron as he sat beside her, chatting with Eli about some project in the woodshop.

Perhaps she was getting ahead of herself. In all likelihood, the flowers were merely a friendly gift and her grandfather had misread Aaron's intentions. There was no reason for her to worry about heartache right now, especially when Aaron hadn't made any declaration of romantic intentions.

I'll cross that bridge when I come to it, Grace concluded, though she was nearly certain that she'd never again find herself on the path to courtship.

Chapter Eleven

$\sim$

Aaron was pleased to see that Grace had recovered from her terrible headache. He had trouble thinking of anything but her as he and Eli carried on with their woodworking after the noon meal concluded. He was glad that she'd enjoyed the wildflowers he brought her, but he longed to give her so much more. What fun it would be to take her for a game at the local miniature golf course or to browse at the Bird-in-Hand Farmers' Market. Even the idea of escorting Grace to a singing or some other event for *die youngie* sounded fun to shy, timid Aaron, yet he'd never get the chance to do any of those things with her if he didn't make his move.

At the end of the day, once all of the tools had been cleaned and returned to their proper storage space, Aaron said a quick farewell to Eli. "I'm gonna stop at the *haus* and say goodbye to Grace too," he added as he made a beeline toward the exit.

"Is that all you're gonna say to her?"

When Aaron's only reply came as a shrug, Eli's hearty laughter bounced off the walls of the woodshop.

Aaron hurried outside, squinting against the late afternoon sun as he made his way toward the cottage. He took several deep breaths in a failed attempt to soothe his nerves, wishing that the muggy air was more refreshing. He scur-ried past the flower beds, overflowing with bubblegum-pink petunias that Grace had planted shortly following her arrival in town. It was impossible for Aaron not to notice Grace's handiwork everywhere he looked. He swallowed against the lump that had lodged in his throat, realizing how painful it would be to see these little signs of Grace should she turn down his invitation of courtship, or even worse, decide to terminate their friendship.

Don't you dare chicken out, Aaron scolded himself as he sprinted up the porch stairs. If there was even a sliver of a chance that he could win Grace's heart, he had to take it. He lunged up to the screen door, fearing that he'd change his mind once again if he wasted any time in seeking out Eli's granddaughter.

Aaron burst into the fragrant kitchen, accidentally slamming the screen door in the process.

Grace was stirring a pot on the stove and jumped at the commotion. "*Ach*!" She covered her heart with her free hand.

"S-sorry," Aaron stammered as he rubbed the back of his neck. He sniffed the delightfully fruity scent that lin-gered in the air. "What are you making?"

"Blueberry jam." Grace grinned as she continued to stir the pot. "It's awful hot, but you can try some if you'd like."

"Sure." Aaron scooted to Grace's side. She dipped a clean teaspoon into the pot, then carefully transferred the spoon to Aaron. "Better let that cool for a minute."

"*Jah, gut* idea." Aaron stood there staring awkwardly, holding the spoon at arm's length and staring at Grace. She was flushed from the heat of the day mixed with the warmth of the stove, but she was just as beautiful as the bouquet of wildflowers on the table.

Grace gazed at Aaron with a questioning expression. "Did you smell the jam all the way out in the woodshop? Is that why you ran in here?"

"*Nee*, but it does smell *appenditlich*. I actually... I... uh... I wanted to talk to you about something." He spooned the jam into his mouth to buy himself some time, though it was still nearly too hot to taste. "Very *gut*," he replied as he returned the teaspoon to Grace.

"*Denki*," she replied as she tossed the teaspoon into the sink. "What did you want to talk about?"

Aaron was so nervous that his eyes nearly started to water. Never in his wildest dreams did he think he'd find himself in this position. He'd given up on finding love after several failed attempts at courtship, yet here he was, about to confess his interest to his employer's beautiful granddaughter. Feeling more vulnerable than a newborn pup, he exhaled forcefully, unable to hide his anxiety behind his shaky breath.

"Is everything *oll recht*?" Grace asked, nervously splitting her gaze between Aaron and the pot she was still stirring.

"I would like to court you," Aaron blurted out so quickly that his words blended all into one.

There. He'd said it. No turning back now.

Grace let out a soft gasp. She dropped her wooden spoon to the floor, splattering sticky purple jam onto the floor. "What did you just say?"

Aaron watched the spoon as it fell, though to him it seemed to move in slow motion. Once the spoon hit the floor, he looked back up at Grace and pressed on. "I've been thinking about… I've been wanting for us to have this conversation for a while now, but the timing has never been right. I'd always lose my courage, or I couldn't catch you alone."

Grace stared at him, her eyes opened wide, appearing as huge blue marbles.

Aaron could not hear the sound of the jam starting to bubble over the sound of his own heartbeat. Why wasn't Grace saying anything? Was she stunned that he brought this up, or was she perhaps scrambling to find the words that would turn him down as gently as possible? Was she bubbling over with rage, just like the near-boiling jam, at the fact that Aaron insisted on bringing up the topic of romance when she'd so vehemently spoken against it in the not-too-distant past?

"I don't think I could live with myself if I didn't tell you that I'm interested in growing our relationship beyond friendship," he concluded softly, hanging his head.

"*Ach*, Aaron," Grace muttered as she released a pent-up breath. She glanced around the room and wrung her hands together. "I don't know if… I'm not sure what to say. I'm not sure if I'm ready for—"

"That's okay," Aaron stopped her, holding his hand in the air. "You don't have to say anymore." He turned to leave, though he wanted to run as fast as his legs could carry him. Heat crept up his neck as he considered what a fool he'd made of himself. He thought he'd become immune to embarrassment over his twenty-five years of living life as a socially awkward person, but nothing could have prepared him for the humiliation that seared through him now. "I just hope this hasn't ruined our friendship," he mumbled over his shoulder before scurrying toward the door.

"Hang on," Grace called after his retreating form. "I'm not saying no."

Aaron screeched to a halt and spun around. "You're not?"

Grace shook her head, her mouth agape. She rubbed her hands on her apron, then bent to retrieve the dropped spoon. "There are some serious things we need to discuss before I can truly give you an answer." She dampened a paper towel and then leaned over to wipe up droplets of jam from the floor.

The wavering yet catchy tune of an old man's humming floated through the open window. Eli was headed for the house, and their moment of privacy was about to come to an end.

"Let's meet where Muddy Run meets the road on Saturday at ten o'clock," Grace said under her breath. "I'll just say I'm going for a walk, and then we can talk more freely."

"*Jah*, okay. Saturday at ten." Aaron pinched his eyes shut to collect himself. He was resigned to the fact that whatever Grace needed to get off her chest couldn't be said just now. Exhausted by the effort it took to be so vulnerable, he forced himself to open his eyes. "See you later."

After his quick farewell to Grace, he said a second goodbye to Eli, whom he'd crossed paths with on the porch. Aaron made his way to the stable to hitch up his horse and buggy, and once sheltered by the privacy of the small barn, he bent over, placed his hand on his knees, and took several deep breaths.

Straightening back up to his full height, he took off his

straw hat and ruffled his hair to release some nervous energy. Even though Grace hadn't turned down his request to court her, having to wait nearly a week to continue their delicate conversation filled him with dread. Though he was plagued with countless uncertainties that swarmed through his mind like a cloud of mosquitoes, the chance to win Grace's heart was worth the wait, and that was something that he was certain of.

Grace hurried along the shoulder of North Weavertown Road on Saturday morning, the silky overgrown grass tickling the bottoms of her bare feet as she walked. She glanced up at the overcast sky, noticing a collection of slate-gray clouds on the horizon. She could almost smell a summer storm in the air, and she was thankful for it, hoping that a good, steady rain shower would break up some of the August mugginess. Hopefully, the inclement weather would hold off until she and Aaron had concluded their rendezvous, but getting caught in the rain didn't entirely sound all that unpleasant.

She smiled to herself as she skirted past a herd of Jersey cattle that were grazing contentedly in their pasture. She recalled how much she enjoyed rainy days as a child, stomping and splashing in puddles with her siblings and catching raindrops on her tongue. Her smile faded as she wondered if she'd ever experience that childlike joy again. It was almost as if a piece of the person she'd once been had been erased following her first love's betrayal, and if she had to guess, that piece of her had been lost forever.

Pushing that pitiful thought out of her mind, Grace noticed a young Amish man seated in the grass as the narrow creek came into view. She quickened her pace, surprised that Aaron had beaten her to their meeting place, considering that there was no buggy in sight and the walk to Muddy Run was considerably longer for him than it was for her.

"I hope I'm not late," Grace called as she sprinted up to him, taking a moment to catch her breath. "No buggy today?"

Aaron, who'd been staring at the babbling creek, looked over at her and offered a wave that almost seemed uncertain. "I thought a walk would do me good and help to clear my head." He motioned for her to take a seat on the bank beside him.

Sensing Aaron's unease, Grace suddenly felt terribly guilty for asking him to wait almost a week to continue their heart-to-heart conversation. She'd also felt uncomfortable knowing that she'd soon have to verbally recall a time in her life that was best left forgotten. But Aaron was still at least somewhat in the dark, and Grace could imagine how fretful the past several days must have been for him.

Lowering herself onto the grass beside him, she dipped her feet into the creek, relishing the feeling of the cool water. "I'm sorry if I kept you waiting today, and that we had to wait all week for a private time to talk. I hope I didn't make you *naerfich*."

"That's okay, I'm always *naerfich* anyway."

Grace chuckled at Aaron's open remark, knowing that there was plenty of truth behind it. She sighed, feeling her stomach sour at the memories that she was about to relive. She took in the scenic view before them, a sea of lush greenness as grazing pastures collided with neighboring fields of cornstalks and soybeans. The sounds of the nearby herd of cattle lowing to each other as they grazed mixed with the liquid melody of the creek as it babbled over countless smooth stones. Yet even amid the beauty of God's creation, Grace was troubled.

"When I was a little *maedel*, I had a friend named Ben Zook," she started, as she ran her fingers through the grass. "Some of the other *maed* teased me that I was friends with a *bu*, but it didn't matter what they said because Ben and I just clicked. His family's farm neighbors ours, so we took advantage of every opportunity to play together." Her fingers grazed over something hard in the grass. Separating the blades, she pulled out a small rock and then grasped it tightly as she continued. "We went for rides in his pony cart every day that the sun was shining and we convinced my *daed* to put up a second rope swing in our barn so we didn't have to take turns. We'd ride our scooters up and down the lane and sometimes we'd even help each other with our chores so we could get to our playtime that much faster."

"Sounds like he was a real *gut freind*," Aaron commented, his concern poorly masked on his face.

"*Jah*, for sure and for certain." Grace ran her fingers over the stone as she recalled that happy time in her life. "I developed a crush on Ben as we grew older, but I never said a word about it. After all, I couldn't risk scaring my best friend away."

Aaron said nothing, though the straight line of his mouth twisted into a grimace.

"I looked forward to my sixteenth birthday so I could start attending gatherings for *die youngie*," Grace went on, rotating the stone against her palm. "I hoped that Ben might ask to court me, but I forced myself not to get my hopes up." She rolled her eyes at the memory. "Imagine my surprise when Ben pulled me aside on my sixteenth birthday and said he'd been waiting for that day so he could ask me to be his *aldi*."

Aaron's frown deepened. "He must've really fancied you if he was also counting the days down until you were sixteen."

"I thought so too," Grace whispered before she pitched the rock into the creek. "We courted for seven years, and during that time he made several comments about our future as *mann* and *fraa*."

"So, you were betrothed?"

"*Nee*, not officially, but I assumed a proposal was coming because Ben acted like it was." Tears gathered in her eyes, but she refused to shed them. Blinking rapidly to keep them at bay, she went on. "It sounds *narrish*, but as time went on, I became more and more certain that we'd marry. I mean, who courts for seven years without getting hitched?"

She let out another sigh, this one almost as heavy as the gray sky above. The storm that was brewing nearby matched the unsettledness within her. The gentle breeze soon strengthened into a gust, causing the ribbons of her kapp to blow against her cheek. Grace wondered what would fall first, raindrops or teardrops.

"One day I received a letter from Ben. He'd written that we had some awful important things to discuss. He asked me to meet him that Sunday night at the line of maple trees that separated our *familye* farms." She snickered, recalling her naivety. "I thought that a proposal was coming. The tone of his letter was so serious, and he'd asked to meet at one of our favorite spots, so what else could he have wanted to discuss?"

"*Jah*, that makes sense," Aaron agreed.

"So, when Sunday night came, I tiptoed out of the house when everyone was asleep and met Ben under the cover of nightfall. I thought it was ever so romantic, but when I saw his face, I knew that something was wrong."

"What happened?" Aaron asked, placing a hand on his hat to keep it from blowing off.

Grace shuddered, though her shivering wasn't caused by the strengthening wind. "He told me that he never had feelings for me and only courted me because it was expected of him."

Aaron's jaw dropped. "That's *baremlich*, Grace. You didn't deserve to be led on like that."

"Adding to my shock, Ben admitted to being deeply unsatisfied with Plain life and told me that he was leaving our community to pursue a career as a musician. He told me he'd left a note for his family and would be leaving that very night."

Aaron stared at her in disbelief. "Had he already joined the church?"

"*Jah*, he had taken the kneeling vow the summer before, after dragging his feet for quite some time. I tried to remind him of his commitment to *Gott* and our church, but he insisted that he'd made a mistake when choosing to be baptized. He said he'd accept a shunning if it was imposed on him, which it was after he sent a letter to our bishop, renouncing his faith." She pinched her eyes shut, sending large teardrops rolling down her cheeks. "In one night, I lost the man I loved and my best friend."

Aaron reached over and wiped her tears away with his calloused fingers. "I'm so sorry, Grace. I can't imagine how *baremlich* that must've been."

She forced a smile, pained as it was, relishing his comforting touch. "It was so devastating that I vowed I'd never start courting again."

Aaron pulled his hand away from her cheek and then looked away. "I can understand why you'd feel that way," he quietly replied after a very lengthy pause.

Grace could barely hear what he'd said over the wind ripping through nearby cornstalks and a sudden rumble of thunder, yet the dejected look on his face cried out to her heart. She longed to inch closer and wrap her arms around him, perhaps even rest her head on his broad shoulder, but she thought it too forward.

"But then I met you," she stated, "and that made me reconsider my vow."

Aaron's head spun to face her, reminding Grace of a barn owl. "Really?"

She grinned, pleased to see sunshine returning to his previously gloomy expression. "I've seen what a *gut* man you are and I would like to be courted by you, but I need things to move slowly. I'm... I'm having trouble trusting that I won't get hurt again. Sometimes I think that maybe the Lord's plan for my life doesn't include falling in love again."

"*Ach*, I'm sure that's not the case." Aaron clasped one of her hands in both of his. "Anyone with a heart like yours deserves to be loved."

Grace sniffled as she looked at her hand that was wrapped safely in his. She felt the warmth of a blush spread across her cheeks as she took in Aaron's sincere, reassuring words.

"I'll do my best to never disappoint you as your first beau did," he continued, giving her hand a little squeeze, his chocolate-colored eyes locked on her. "And it's *gut* that we will take things slowly. You'll need to be patient with me since I've no experience in being a beau."

They shared a laugh that was interrupted by a much louder clap of thunder that shook the ground they sat on.

"We better get outta here before the lightning finds us," Aaron said, releasing Grace's hand as he scrambled to his feet.

Grace rose more slowly, shaking the wrinkles out of her skirt. "Why don't you come back to the cottage? It's closer than your place, and maybe we can convince *Daadi* to play a game of Scrabble with us."

Aaron tipped his head upward and studied the dark rain clouds that were liable to burst open at any minute. "*Jah*, that sounds much better than getting caught outside in the storm. Let's go!"

With that they took off on foot, sprinting down the quiet lane and dodging the first raindrops as they fell. They ran as fast as their legs could carry them, like two overgrown children playing tag in the yard of the schoolhouse.

Grace was secretly thankful for this chance to stretch their legs, both of them too winded to carry on a conversation as they darted toward the cottage. She was still in disbelief that she'd agreed to be Aaron's sweetheart, yet his soft-spoken, thoughtful ways had certainly made an impression on her, and even caused a stirring in her soul. If she gave Aaron her fragile heart, could she trust him not to break it?

I hope I made the right decision. Grace's brief thought was covered in a sticky coating of worry, though she knew that only time would tell.

Chapter Twelve

"**K**eep those eyes closed," Aaron said with a tickled grin. He kept a tight grip on the reins as his horse and buggy traveled up Peach Lane. He took his eyes off the road to peek over at Grace, who was wearing a pretty smile along with a lovely bubblegum pink dress. It was a dress he'd never seen her wear before, and he wondered if she'd made it especially for their first real date.

"*Ach*, I feel like my eyes have been closed for an hour," she giggled, the color of her cheeks matching the shade of her dress. "Won't you tell me where we're going?"

Aaron shook his head and then realized Grace couldn't see him. "Nope, you'll just have to wait and see when we get there, but you're *wilkumme* to guess."

"*Vell*, I'm thinking we're over near Strasburg because I heard us cross over the railroad tracks."

"That we did, but we're not exactly headed for the village of Strasburg," Aaron said as he slowed the horse to a walk as they approached a fairly steep hill. "But we're almost there, so you won't have to hold your breath for too much longer."

"You said nothing about holding my breath. You only told me to close my eyes," Grace replied with a feisty smile, her eyelashes fluttering against her cheek as if she was dying to look around.

Aaron chuckled at their friendly banter, feeling blessed to have such a good-natured, attractive young woman beside him. A flicker of disbelief threatened to ignite, and he wondered why a woman like Grace would be interested in courting someone as introverted and awkward as himself. Had she only agreed to go out with him out of pity? What if things went south between them? Then he would not only lose the girl but maybe also his shot at taking over Eli's business.

Grace made another guess as to where they were headed, and Aaron's focus shifted back to their conversation. Her second guess was also incorrect, but it didn't matter since they'd arrived at their destination.

"Just a minute while I tend to the horse and pay for our entry," Aaron said to Grace as he slid out of the buggy.

"Admission? We must be doing something fancy," Grace commented rather loudly, leaning toward the buggy's open front window.

Aaron smirked as he tied the horse to a nearby fence post. "I wouldn't be caught dead going anywhere fancy." He enjoyed the melodic sound of Grace's laugh as he dashed away to pay for their admission. When he returned, he instructed his date to keep her eyes closed as he helped her down from the buggy and led her about a dozen yards forward. He'd been planning this moment ever since Grace had agreed to their courtship and everything needed to be just perfect. After all, this very moment might be the start of a lifelong love story!

"Okay," Aaron said as he gently turned Grace to face the proper direction. "You can open your eyes now." He stood to her side, nearly shaking with the giddiness of a young child on Christmas morning. He'd taken her to the Wildflower Lookout, which was a breathtaking spectacle of the Lord's creation. Located on a Plain family farm, the vista was situated on the top of a hill where several acres of wildflowers covered the ground. Colorful blossoms dotted the landscape like sprinkles on a birthday cake. The beauty of nature and farmland stretched for as far as the eye could see, and Aaron hoped that Grace would feel as close to the Creator as he did when taking in the scenery.

Grace opened her eyes and her smile dropped. She took in a quick breath as she glanced around the fields of wildflowers, though her furrowed eyebrows and pained expression seemed to express disappointment instead of awe.

"Is everything *oll recht*?" Aaron asked, feeling his heart sink to the pit of his stomach. "I thought you'd like to come here since you seemed to enjoy the bouquet I gave you recently."

Grace's pout quickly bounced back into a smile, albeit an obviously forced grin. "*Jah*, of course. *Denki* for bringing me." She briefly hung her head before looking away from Aaron and gesturing toward the narrow walking trail. "Let's go enjoy all of these *blumme*."

Aaron hurried to catch up with her as she took several quick steps forward. He tried to get a peek at her face as they ambled side by side through the winding, dirt path, though it was no easy task. It was almost as if Grace was going out of her way to hide her face.

Did she expect more from our first official date, or is she regretting that she agreed to court me? Aaron silently fretted as a sudden sensation of nausea swept through him.

Something was definitely off, and the fact that he couldn't put his finger on what had gone wrong was unsettling.

"I'm glad we have such beautiful weather today," Aaron blurted to break the uncomfortable silence. "A stroll through the *blumme* wouldn't be nearly as nice on a rainy day."

Grace nodded and remained silent.

Aaron held in a groan, hoping that some small talk would have lightened the suddenly strained mood. He adjusted the brim of his hat, needing to fiddle with something. "What is your favorite kind of flower?"

"*Ach*, I don't know," Grace mumbled, her eyes fixed on her feet instead of the glorious surroundings. "I think I like sunflowers the best, but I also like daffodils."

"We may see some sunflowers today, but you'll have to wait until spring for the daffodils," Aaron replied, doing his best to keep their conversation alive.

"*Jah*."

"So, your favorite color must be yellow."

"*Jah*."

"Nice. Bright and cheerful." Aaron shoved his hands into his pockets, almost chuckling at the irony of the statement. Even despite his attempts at making conversation, Grace seemed intent on clamming up. What in the world had gone wrong between them in a matter of seconds?

He mentally dissected every moment of their day as they strolled through the flowers in silence, trying to pinpoint anything that could have derailed their otherwise pleasant outing, and possibly their relationship.

Grace gasped, startling Aaron out of his thoughts. "*Wass iss letz?*"

"Look who we almost stepped on." Grace pointed to

a tiny, brown field mouse that was frozen in fear on the path in front of them. The little critter was no bigger than a blackberry, and as they inched closer he trembled like an autumn leaf on a windy day. "*Ach*, poor thing. He's only a *boppli, jah*?"

"Seems like it," Aaron agreed, watching as Grace scooped the little animal into her hand. "His *mamm* probably isn't too far away."

Grace's eyes narrowed as she scanned the nearby area. "Look," she whispered, tilting her head toward the edge of the path, where wildflowers mingled with the waist-high grass. A larger mouse was peeking out of the dense brush, waiting to see what these giants were doing with her baby.

Grace tiptoed over to the mother mouse who shrunk back into the grass. "Here's your *boppli*," she cooed as she lowered her hand and allowed the baby mouse to hop down. "Keep an eye on him so he doesn't stray back onto the path."

The mother mouse soon turned and scampered off into the tangle of grass and flowers with her baby following closely behind.

Watching the sweet scene unfold gave Aaron a warm, fuzzy feeling. "Most women run away from *meis*," he pointed out, a cautious grin returning to his face.

"I've always had a heart for animals," Grace said, her expression soft as cotton candy. "Even when I was a little *maedel*, I would find mice caught in glue traps and free them using a dab of cooking oil. One time my *mamm* nearly fainted when she saw me giving one a bath in the kitchen sink," she chuckled at the childhood memory.

"You have a *gut* heart," Aaron said with unfamiliar confidence, knowing that there were heaps of truth behind the compliment. "When we find a *maus* in our *haus*, I'm always the one *Mamm* calls on to catch them. I'm usually quick enough to snatch them up and carry them outside. I can't stand the thought of any animal suffering in a trap."

"That's sweet, and a little funny to picture." Grace shielded her growing smile with her fingers, though Aaron secretly wished she wouldn't hide the lovely sight. "We both have a heart for *Gott*'s creatures, *jah*?" Her hand brushed against his as they continued walking side by side. "Every time we talk, we find out that we have more in common."

"*Jah*, sure seems like it." He felt her hand knock lightly against his for a second time. If only that odd hiccup in their outing hadn't happened earlier, he might have felt bold enough to take her hand in his.

Aaron was pleased that he and Grace had moved past the unexpected coldness that had wafted between them earlier, but it still troubled him that she had seemed almost on the verge of tears, even if for a short time. He knew he wouldn't be able to enjoy the rest of their outing unless he learned what had upset Grace and how he could avoid such an incident in the future.

"There's a bench over yonder. Should we sit and enjoy the scenery for a bit?"

Grace's suggestion shook Aaron out of his thoughts. He glanced in the direction that she was pointing and saw the iron bench that was shaded from behind by a row of lofty sunflowers.

"*Jah*, that sounds nice," he agreed. As they headed toward the secluded seat, he decided that though he wasn't bold enough to take her hand, he was daring enough to ask about the uncomfortable moment that they'd shared at the start of their walk. Besides, he refused to allow the possibility of a thorny conversation to uproot the beautiful thing that was growing between them.

As Grace lowered herself onto the bench, she closed her eyes and took in a slow, deep breath, enjoying the fresh country air that was perfumed with subtle floral notes. She tilted her face upward, allowing the sun to warm her cheeks. A pair of robins flew overhead, tweeting a song that mixed with the sweet melody of young children's laughter. Grace opened her eyes and her lips curled into a smile as she watched the young *Englisch* family in the distance, both parents snapping photos of their toddler girls as they clumsily sniffed a large red zinnia.

Her thorough enjoyment of the stunning surroundings was suddenly interrupted when she felt the sensation of being watched. Having become accustomed to tourists snapping photos of her and others in her Plain community, Grace slowly turned to ask Aaron if he had the feeling of eyes on him. She jumped slightly then chuckled when she realized it had been Aaron who was staring at her.

"*Ach*, you startled me," she said with a giggle. Her content grin faded when she noticed the firm set of his jaw. "Is…is everything *oll recht*?"

A smile crept onto his face that didn't reach his dark eyes. "I was just gonna ask you the same question. I was wondering if you're having a *gut* time."

Grace's eyebrows rose. "*Jah*, of course. It's a sunny day and I'm in a *schee* place with my new beau." Her eyes darted down to his hands, which were clasped tightly together. "Are *you* having a nice time?"

"For the most part, *jah*." His knuckles cracked as he

wrung his hands together. "Though if I'm being honest, I have to admit that I'm a little worried."

Grace didn't have the heart to tell him that his deep frown was giving away his thoughts more than his words did. "Why is that?"

"I saw the look on your face when you opened your eyes and realized where I'd brought you." The right side of his mouth turned upward. "It wasn't exactly a happy look."

Grace felt like her heart had been punctured by a quilting needle. She was slightly stunned to learn that Aaron had such a strong reaction to what she thought was only a temporary setback in their day. On top of that, she was annoyed with herself for letting the past creep into the present. After all, Aaron couldn't have possibly known of the significance this place held.

"Grace?"

"My former beau also brought me here on our first date," she quietly admitted. "We came here quite often throughout the years that we courted." She sighed as she felt her eyes starting to well up, and she blinked rapidly, refusing to give in to yet another round of tears over Ben's betrayal. "I never thought I'd come here again, so it was a bit of a shock when I opened my eyes and saw this place."

Aaron leaned forward and hung his head. "I'm such a *dummkopp*."

Grace hated to hear Aaron talk so poorly of himself. "*Nee*, you're not. Please don't ever say that."

Aaron rubbed his forehead, his eyes narrowing into thin slits. "*Jah*, but I could have asked you what you wanted to do today instead of scheming behind your back."

"Planning a surprise that you think your *aldi* will enjoy is hardly scheming, Aaron." She gingerly placed her hand on his broad shoulder and briefly petitioned the Lord, asking that his spirit might be strengthened to match his physical brawn. "If you can't be kinder to yourself, I don't think we'll be able to continue our courtship."

Aaron glanced at her hand, still resting on his upper arm. His eyes met hers and his face reddened. "I won't allow that, for sure and for certain."

They shared a soft, knowing grin that caused Grace's heart to flutter.

"I just feel *baremlich* that I unknowingly brought up old wounds by bringing you here," Aaron stated as an orange-and-black monarch butterfly flitted past. "I'm sorry."

"There's no reason to apologize. You didn't do anything wrong." She removed her hand from his shoulder and watched with amusement as the butterfly turned back toward them.

Having taken a liking to Aaron, the butterfly circled him several times before landing on top of his hat. It remained there for a moment before crawling down around the brim, then across his cheek, and finally to the bridge of his nose. As if settling in, the colorful bug spread its wings to absorb the warmth of the sun.

Aaron sat as still as a statue, letting the butterfly rest on his nose. His eyes crossed as he stared at the butterfly, holding his breath so the dainty insect wouldn't startle and fly away.

The simple, precious sight unfolding before her was nearly enough to cause happy tears to well up in Grace's eyes. She beamed, seeing Aaron's gentle, meek ways in a new light. Sure, her heart was growing fonder of him every day, though now she felt a stirring of something that both thrilled and terrified her.

"You know, despite the memories that initially flooded me when I realized where we were, I'm very glad to be in this place again…with you," she said just above a whisper. "*Denki* again for bringing me here."

Aaron peered at her past the butterfly's wings. "*Denki* for coming with me." He slowly raised his hand, extended his pointer finger, and waited while the butterfly crawled onto it. "Hold your hand out," he said as he moved his hand toward hers at a snail's pace.

Grace held out her pointer finger and tried to remain as still as possible as the butterfly moseyed from its perch on Aaron's finger onto hers. His finger bumped against hers ever so lightly, but it was enough to nearly take Grace's breath away. Try as she might, she couldn't focus on the lovely butterfly now, not when her heart was racing and she longed for Aaron to take her hand in his, or better yet, wrap her in an embrace that would never end.

Doing her best to take a deep yet inconspicuous breath, Grace lowered her hand as the butterfly flapped its wings and went on its way, weaving its flight path between the clusters of daisies, cosmos, and poppies. There was no denying it; she had more than a passing interest in Aaron King. As implausible as it sounded, she was falling in love with him. She'd need to pray often and fervently for the Lord to bless her new relationship with Aaron.

Chapter Thirteen

Grace hadn't been able to stop smiling since her date with Aaron. She found herself grinning from ear to ear as she weeded Eli's vegetable garden and hummed energetic melodies as she fed the damp laundry through the wringers in the gas-powered washing machine. She continued to make lunch for her grandfather and Aaron, and enjoyed sharing the meal with them too, though she secretly longed for more one-on-one time with her handsome, soft-spoken beau. Each day that passed felt brighter and more hopeful than the last, and the wall that she'd built around her heart lowered more and more as the days turned into weeks.

When Grace began to prepare breakfast one September morning, she noticed that the small pantry looked bare. After the meal was served and the dishes washed, she jotted down a shopping list, hitched Eli's mare to the buggy, and made the short trip to Kauffman's Fruit Farm and Market.

Grace leisurely pushed a shopping cart down the aisles of the small, family-owned market, enjoying the soothing hymns that played from the store's speakers. The delightful scent of apples heavily perfumed the store, and she marveled at the many locally grown varieties to choose from. She placed a small container of blackberries into the cart, thinking that she could whip up a pitcher of black-berry lemonade to enjoy with Eli and Aaron.

As she moved into the aisle of bulk snacks and baking ingredients, she reached into her handbag in search of her list, not wanting to forget any items she needed. As she rummaged through the bag, she heard another shopper and their cart approaching.

"Grace! How *wunderbaar gut* to see you."

She looked up and saw Becky King headed toward her, wearing a rose-colored dress that matched the shade of her plump cheeks.

"*Guder mariye,*" Grace politely greeted Aaron's mother with a smile. "It's nice to see you as well. Did Annie come shopping with you today?"

Becky scoffed and threw her hands in the air, though her smile remained steady. "That *dochder* of mine stayed home to play with the *busslin* instead of helping her *mamm* with the shopping. I don't know what she's going to do when those critters are fully grown and go to new homes."

Grace was tickled at the thought of Annie trying to wrangle the busy kittens as they grew older and more in-dependent. "Oh, to be a *kind* again, *jah*?"

Becky nodded enthusiastically. "Carefree and full of wonder." She glanced into her shopping cart, which con-tained several packages of sugar and flour. "I've got a lot of baking to do. I'm hosting a Sisters' Day this com-ing Saturday and need to bake plenty of sweets to serve. You're more than *wilkumme* to join us for some sisterly fellowship."

"*Denki*, I would like that very much," Grace replied, pleased to be included. "Should I bring anything?"

"Only yourself and some empty jars. We're gonna make gallons of applesauce."

They chatted for a few more minutes about different recipes for applesauce and the large variety of apples that were for sale before saying farewell and continuing with their shopping.

Grace pushed her shopping cart past Aaron's mother and took another look at her shopping list. "Sugar, flour, and baking soda," she whispered to herself, then began scanning the shelves for the best deals.

"Sorry to bother you again," Becky said meekly as she approached Grace for a second time. "The Lord has laid something on my heart, and I think it should be shared with you."

"A message from *Gott* is never a bother," Grace replied with a genuine grin, "and neither is a chat with a friend."

Becky smiled at that, though she seemed a bit more subdued than her usual bubbly self. "I… I wanted to say *denki*."

"For what?"

"For the effect you've had on my *sohn*." Becky's dark brown eyes welled up and her lips quivered ever so slightly. "Aaron's always been a quiet, timid one, and for years his *daed* and I worried about him." She swiped away a tear before it could roll down her cheek. "But since you've come into his life, he's slowly become more outgoing. He's been more talkative, and he's sharing his thoughts without being asked. It feels like we're getting to know our *sohn* for the first time, twenty-five years after his birth."

Grace placed her hand over her heart, moved by the details that Aaron's mother had shared with her. "I pray daily for everyone in my life, but I can hardly take credit for—"

"Then it was your prayers on his behalf," Becky interjected as she brushed away another joyful tear.

"But I didn't ask *Gott* to change Aaron," Grace persisted. "I just asked *Gott* to bless him and keep him from harm."

"*Jah*, but your talks with *Gott* brought my *sohn* to His mind, and He knows just what each one of us needs to thrive." Becky cleared her throat, glanced down at her shopping cart, then back up at Grace. "I won't take up any more of your time. See you on Saturday."

Grace stood motionless as Becky went on her way, overcome by the woman's meaningful words. She had seen Aaron coming out of his shell with her own eyes, but hearing that he was becoming more outgoing directly from the woman who'd raised him deeply moved Grace. Seeing Aaron's confidence grow filled her heart with gladness, and she knew only good things would come from it.

Do others see a change in me since I met Aaron? Grace knew the answer to the question she'd asked herself. The gloom that hovered over her since her former beau's betrayal had lifted, and she found herself smiling for no reason quite often. *Daadi* had recently commented on her more positive outlook. Letters from her family and friends back in Paradise also expressed that they noticed a more peaceful tone in her written correspondence since she moved to Bird-in-Hand.

What would life be like if Aaron and I got married? Grace wondered as she resumed her shopping. She stared at the display of seasonings and spices, though she wasn't truly seeing the selection of flavorings. If things continued going the way they were between her and Aaron, a wedding might not be that far off. The idea of living her life as

Mrs. Aaron King pleased her to no end, and she imagined the contented life they would lead as husband and wife.

Let's not put the cart before the horse, Grace thought as she smiled at her vivid thoughts. *If Aaron and I are meant to wed, it will happen in the Lord's timing.* Feeling more hopeful than ever, she placed a container of salt into her shopping cart, then pushed it into the next aisle.

After Aaron had finished his Saturday morning chores around his family's farm, he made his way to the front yard with a bucket of paint in one hand and a paintbrush and flat-head screwdriver in the other. His mother had asked him to repaint the wooden picket fence that surrounded her vegetable garden, and since the sky had threatened rain most of the week, today was the perfect day to complete the job.

Aaron knelt in the grass near the fence and pried the lid off the paint can, then dipped his brush into the white paint. He glanced toward the house when a chorus of feminine laughter rang through the open windows. His mother was hosting a Sisters' Day, and the house was full of female relatives, friends, and neighbors. He suspected Grace would be in attendance, though he hadn't seen any sign of her yet.

He beamed as he swiped the paintbrush across the fence, thinking of his great affection for his boss's granddaughter. True, her turquoise eyes, lightly freckled cheeks, and lovely smile were very pleasant to look at, but it was Grace's tender spirit and empathetic ways that had captured Aaron's attention. The more time he spent with her, the more he yearned for her presence. Spending time with Grace felt like the first mild day of spring after a bitterly cold winter, and Aaron wondered how he'd managed to muddle through day-to-day life before she'd arrived in Bird-in-Hand.

The clip-clopping of iron horseshoes and the creaking of buggy wheels that needed to be oiled interrupted his musings. He looked over his shoulder and immediately recognized Eli's horse by the white star-shaped marking on the animal's muzzle. He waved, balanced his brush across the rim of the paint can, then rose to meet the buggy.

As Aaron reached the edge of the lawn, Grace hopped out of the buggy before it came to a halt, slung a cloth tote bag over her shoulder, and dashed for the house. "Hello and goodbye," she called with a chuckle. "I'm running late!" She brushed past him, darted across the lawn, then into the house to join the other women.

Aaron stepped up to the buggy, greeted Eli, then gestured toward the house with his thumb. "She's not late. She's right on time."

Eli removed one hand from the reins and stroked his beard. "Late for being early, I reckon, but that's our Gracie."

"*Jah*, she's a special one." Aaron struggled to control his grin, fearing that if he smiled too broadly, he might burst into a fit of laughter. He was so thoroughly jubilant, and surprised, to call a woman like Grace his *aldi* that his delight sometimes manifested in fits of hilarity.

Smiling like a cat who'd just captured a mouse, Eli leaned toward Aaron. "It's *gut* to see that look on your face."

"What look?"

"The look of a man who's in *lieb*," Eli answered, his crackling voice a little too loud for Aaron's comfort.

Love? Was he in love? Aaron's vision started to spin

as the weight of Eli's observation crashed into him like an angry bull. He'd come to care for Grace immensely, but did that equal love? Sure, she occupied nearly every moment of his thoughts and each second of his dreams. He often wondered if their future children would inherit her lovely blue eyes, and he pictured them sitting in side-by-side rocking chairs in their old age. He knew, without a doubt that he'd give his life for hers, and that she made him feel more content and peaceful than he'd ever known was possible.

I do love her. I love Grace Ebersol.

The realization threatened to knock him off his feet but a bit of movement in his peripheral vision caught his attention before he could ponder it further. Normally the sight of his favorite sibling would be a welcomed one, but at that moment, Annie's curiosity was the last thing he needed. If she learned that her big brother was in love, she might unintentionally spill the beans before Aaron could decide how to handle his feelings, and that sounded disastrous.

"Cat got your tongue?" Eli asked, goading Aaron on and seemingly unaware that a third party was now within earshot.

Aaron swiped at the perspiration that had gathered between his eyebrows. "*Jah,* I guess so." He held his breath and watched as Annie drew nearer, cradling one of her beloved kittens like a human baby.

"Truth be told, I've always hoped that you and Gracie might end up together," Eli went on, bobbing his head as if listening to a catchy melody. "Makes me wonder if I should retire from woodworking right now so I can start a career as a matchmaker." He let out a hoot and slapped his knee, causing his mare to pin her ears back at the sudden ruckus.

Aaron cringed and fought to keep a straight face as Annie stepped right up to Eli's buggy, her bare feet wisping through the grass.

"What's so *fannich*?" the child asked as she placed the black-and-white kitten on the buggy's seat beside Eli.

Eli's guffawing subsided as he shot a glance at Aaron. Then he grinned at Annie, his eyes still sparkling with well-meaning mischief. "I was laughing because I heard that the kittens you've been looking after are ready to find new homes, and I thought it must be a joke." He reached over and tapped the underside of her chin, grinning at her as if she were his own granddaughter.

Aaron let out a sigh so strong that it forced him to take a few steps backward, feeling like a balloon that someone had just let the air out of. Eli's quick thinking had spared him from any embarrassment, but he still didn't know just how much Annie had overheard.

Annie frowned and stared longingly at the little ball of fluff as it walked up to Eli and sniffed his clothing. "*Jah*, *Daed* said we only need so many mousers around here, so we need to find *gut* homes for most of the *busslin*." Her shoulders sagged for just a moment before she perked back up. "But *Daed* said I can keep one to keep the *mamm* cat company."

"Is this the one you are keeping?" Eli asked as he stroked the purring kitten's downy head.

"*Jah*. I named her Bang because she runs around awful fast and crashes into things when she can't stop in time."

Eli let loose with a belly laugh, though Aaron was too

riddled with alarm to muster anything more than a tiny smile.

"Do you and Grace want to take one of the *busslin* home? Then I could come and visit it anytime." Annie stared at Eli with puppy dog eyes, pleading with a sweet innocence.

"*Vell*, construction on my new *daadi haus* is nearly done, and once it's finished, Grace will be moving back to Paradise and I'll be going with her. Then you'd have to take a long buggy ride to visit the *bussli*, or we'd have to return it to you," Eli gently responded as he picked up the kitten and handed it back to the child.

Annie spun around and looked up at Aaron, eyes wide and lips pouting. "Grace is leaving Bird-in-Hand so soon? I don't want her to go."

Before Aaron could utter a word, Eli chimed in. "*Vell*, maybe Aaron can change her mind." He winked playfully at Aaron, then returned his free hand to the reins. "I better get back to the woodshop. Lots of paperwork to do. *Mache gute*." He clicked his tongue to signal to his docile horse, and with that, they were off.

Eli's horse and buggy only traveled a few yards when Annie turned to Aaron again. "What did Grace's *daadi* mean when he said he was a matchmaker?"

So, Annie had heard everything, though it was obvious that she didn't fully understand the implications of Eli's joke. Aaron rubbed the back of his neck and racked his brain for a child-friendly explanation, knowing that her questions would not cease until her curiosity was satisfied.

"Aaron? What did he mean?"

"*Ach*, I think he meant that he knew Grace and I were meant to be." His heart lurched into his ribcage upon realizing how that might have sounded. "I mean, meant to be in each other's lives. Meant to be friends."

Annie stared up at him, blinking and mouth slightly agape. "Are me and Grace meant to be friends too?"

"*Jah*, of course."

"That's *gut*, 'cause I don't know what we would do without her," she replied before kissing her kitten on its forehead and scampering off toward the barn.

I couldn't agree more, Aaron thought with an unbridled grin as he moseyed back to the garden fence. He resumed his painting project but was unable to focus on the direction of his brushstrokes. His sister was right. Grace was a steady, warm ray of sunshine who helped everyone around her to thrive, and as far as Aaron was concerned, he needed to make a move that would ensure he would never again see an overcast day.

I love you, Grace Ebersol, and I'm going to ask you to be my wife.

Chapter Fourteen

Though the refreshing morning air still lingered outdoors, the King farmhouse had grown quite warm as the twenty-or-so Amish ladies moved around the spacious first floor, chirping friendly greetings and catching up on each other's lives. Grace knew about half of the women in attendance, having met them during church meetings. She was promptly introduced to the rest of Becky's guests, all of whom readily welcomed her and treated her like a long-lost friend. The women ranged in age from their late teens to their late eighties. Most were relatives, some were neighbors, but all were eager to socialize and whip up more applesauce than any of them had ever seen.

After Becky served all of the ladies some lemonade, meadow tea and some oatmeal raisin cookies, the women got to work. Several small groups formed around the kitchen counter and at the two long folding tables that had been set up in preparation for the job at hand. With so many helping hands, the women made quick work of washing, peeling, coring, and chopping several bushels of honeycrisp apples.

Eventually, all of the apples had been cooked and mashed, though it had taken nearly three hours to get through all of the many batches. The sauce was set aside to finish cooling, then the kitchen was tidied before a tray of lunch meats and cheeses were set out, along with three different types of homemade bread, pickles, broccoli and macaroni salads, and homemade potato chips.

Grace was amused when Annie flew into the house, her cheeks ruddy from her vigorous outdoor play. The girl scanned the room as she snatched a pickle from the platter, her brown eyes shining like two new pennies when they landed on Grace.

"Will you help me fix my hair?" Annie begged as she dashed over, still breathless from her adventures. "It's all *schlappich* now."

"*Jah*, of course." Grace fought off a chuckle, knowing that Annie was more than capable of brushing her locks and styling the traditional low bun. Yet being the only girl among her siblings, she probably longed for the experience of having a sister, and Grace was more than willing to accept that position.

Annie led Grace upstairs to her bedroom, taking the steps two at a time. Grace followed behind her, her heart full and nearly fit to burst. Aaron's mother, and his extended family, had treated her like one of their own. Acting as Annie's honorary elder sister felt perfectly natural. She fit in with the King family, and it would be a pleasure to become part of their kin, though that would only happen if she and Aaron were to marry.

Do I want to become Aaron's wife? The question had only been in Grace's mind for a fraction of a second before her heart told her the answer. *I do. I'm in love with Aaron King.*

The realization that she'd fallen in love for a second time was powerful enough to knock her down the stairs, so she gripped the hand railing tightly as she neared the second floor. She knew she'd been falling for Aaron, and falling hard too, but it wasn't until that moment that she realized the extent of the love she had for this soft-spoken, gentle young man. It dawned on her that the intense affection she had for Aaron was a different kind of love than she'd had for her first beau. This one seemed to be sturdier, surer, and almost certainly mutual.

"This is my room," Annie said as she led Grace into the tidy bedroom. She pointed toward the twin bed that was covered with a pink and white quilt. "Sit there while I grab my comb."

"It's nice and *nett* in here," Grace remarked as she lowered herself onto the bed, enjoying the sunlight that spilled into the room from the two open windows.

"*Mamm* made me redd up in here yesterday," Annie said as she plopped down on the floor at Grace's feet. "I didn't see the point, but *Mamm* said every inch of the house needed to be spic and span for Sisters' Day."

Grace grinned as she pulled the hairpins out of what was left of Annie's hair bun. "It never hurts to tidy up before having guests. What would've happened if I came in here to fix your hair and there were cobwebs in the corners?"

"*Ach*, it wouldn't matter." Annie shrugged as her long cocoa tresses cascaded down her back. "You're pretty much *familye* now, *jah*?"

Grace ran her fingers through Annie's silky hair, working out the largest tangles before using the comb. "*Jah*, I think so too." She bit her tongue to keep from giggling, tickled pink by the deep sense of contentment that spread through her. As she combed Annie's hair and parted it down the middle, she became nearly overwhelmed with gratitude and peace when considering the current state of her life. She'd never imagined herself being this satisfied, and the credit for that belonged to Aaron King, the man she loved.

"Are you gonna stay for supper?" Annie asked, interrupting Grace's daydreaming.

"We haven't even eaten lunch yet," Grace replied with a chuckle as she gathered all of Annie's hair into her hands. "I'll need to head home later and fix supper for my *grossdaadi*, and I don't want to wear out my *wilkumme* here."

"That would never happen," Annie assured her, sitting primly as Grace formed a bun near the nape of her neck. "Besides, your *daadi* could eat supper here too. After all, it was his idea for you and my *bruder* to spend time together, so it's only fair to include him."

Grace was sliding Annie's hair pins into place when she froze, startled by Annie's statement. She inhaled sharply, willing her nerves to settle. Perhaps she'd misheard the girl's statement. "W-what did you just say?"

"It was Eli's idea for you and my *bruder* to become best friends," Annie repeated herself, unaware of Grace's sudden grimace.

So, she hadn't misheard. Her trembling fingers dropped the final hairpin, but she didn't hear it clink against the hardwood floor. She didn't reach for it either, too consumed with dread to function. Still, she clung to a thread of hope that perhaps she'd misunderstood Annie's statement.

"Where did you hear this?" Grace asked, wondering if the girl had possibly imagined the scenario that brought her into their family's lives.

Annie picked up the pin and handed it to Grace over her shoulder, still facing away and waiting for her hairstyle to be finished. "Your *daadi* was talking to Aaron about it right after he dropped you off. He said that he wanted you and Aaron to get together and that he's a matchmaker."

Grace blinked rapidly as the room started to swirl around her. A sudden wave of nausea crashed through her middle as her heart leaped into her throat. *If Daadi played matchmaker, then Aaron isn't truly interested in me.* The deeply troubling thought brought tears to her eyes, and she fought to keep her composure. Somehow, she'd fallen for a man who had no sincere feelings for her for the second time in her life.

I'm such a dummkopp. Grace shook her head as she scolded herself, feeling terribly embarrassed and disappointed in herself for not realizing the truth sooner. *Aaron probably felt like he had to court me since* Daadi *chose him to take over the business. I'm nothing more than an obligation to him.*

"Do you need this pin for my hair?"

Unable to speak, Grace took the pin from Annie and slid it into her hair with trembling fingers. "All done."

Annie leaped up and ran over to the small mirror that hung near the door. She ran her hands over her smooth hair as she gazed at her reflection. "Nice and *nett*, *denki*, Grace!" She darted out of the room and then immediately returned, peeking around the doorframe. "Aren't you gonna come eat lunch now?"

Grace slowly stood, so overcome with emotion that she feared she might faint. "I'm not feeling well."

"Are you *grank*?"

"I n-need to go home," Grace replied, brushing past

Annie and doing her best not to fall apart. She needed to hold back her flood of bitter tears until she could be alone with her agony.

"Grace? Are you *oll recht*?"

She ignored Annie's concern as she swiftly made her way down the stairs. Pleading with the Lord that she would remain unnoticed, she wove her way through the crowded kitchen and slipped out of the screen door.

Once outdoors, Grace was unable to keep her tears at bay. Feeling as if she'd been punched in the stomach, she bent over, placed her hands on her knees, and silently wept. Just mere moments ago she'd felt nearly blissful, realizing that she'd fallen in love, against all odds. It only took a few words from an innocent child to shatter that peaceful, joyful feeling, though she couldn't blame Annie for that. The dear girl had only spoken the truth. It was Aaron who'd tricked Grace into thinking that he cared for her. It was Aaron who knew how tender her heart was, yet chose to knowingly deceive her to gain an established, respected business.

Grace's world felt unstable, like a rickety rope bridge over a raging river, yet one thing was certain. She'd built a fence around her heart after Ben's betrayal, but now that Aaron had deceived her, that fence would need to be re-built as a solid rock wall.

Defeated, dejected, and hopeless, Grace dashed across the lawn and made her way toward the quiet lane, unsure of where she was going, but certain that she didn't care.

Upon realizing that he wouldn't have enough paint to give the garden fence a second coat, Aaron promptly headed for the pasture to collect his horse. He hurried as he led Clove to his buggy, hoping to complete the errand as quickly as possible. Grace was nearby, and he relished every opportunity he had to be close to her, even if it was only to hear her laughter ring out from the kitchen window.

Aaron led the gelding up to the barn, then tied the horse to the hitching rail. He scurried into the barn's tack room to fetch the harness then skedaddled back to his waiting horse. He was in high spirits, having newly realized his love for Grace and deciding that he would ask her to be his bride, so he started to whistle a simple, cheerful tune. It was foreign to him, being so thoroughly content, but Grace and the Lord had worked together to put a song in his heart, and he simply couldn't contain it.

He worked to ready his horse, whistling all the while, but stopped when he thought he heard a woman's voice. He glanced around, and not immediately seeing anyone, he continued hitching his horse. Then the sound came again, this time sounding like a faint yet bitter cry. Was someone weeping? Filled with concern, he scanned his surroundings a second time.

A woman stood near the house, bent over and shuddering as if she'd ventured into a blizzard without a warm coat. Was she ill? Aaron watched with rapt attention, wondering if he should approach her and offer some assistance.

He was able to get a better look at the woman when she straightened her posture, and his heart slammed into his chest when he realized her identity. It was Grace! He watched as she wiped her eyes and then moved across the lawn, weeping into her hands.

"Grace!" he called to her through cupped hands. "Are you *oll recht*?"

She either didn't hear him or chose to ignore him, but

he couldn't imagine her giving him, or anyone, the cold shoulder. She continued toward the road, her pace quickening as she reached the lane.

"Grace! *Wass iss letz*?"

Without breaking her stride, Grace glanced in Aaron's direction. Even with the significant distance between them, Aaron shuddered at the unmistakable look of grief on her face.

What in the world? Aaron was shaken by the deeply troubled expression on Grace's usually smiling face. Why was she crying so pitifully? Why didn't she stop when he'd called out to her? Had she received word that something bad had happened to her grandfather?

His first reaction was to take off on foot after her, but he couldn't leave Clove unattended, partially hitched up for an errand. Frustrated with the task that was separating him from his distraught love, he grumbled to himself as he finished hitching his horse to the carriage. He flung himself into the buggy the moment that the job was done. Not wasting any time, he grabbed the reins and then clicked his tongue to get the horse moving. He hurried Clove out of the barnyard, down the drive, and onto the lane, all with a sinking feeling that something was terribly wrong.

Aaron kept a white-knuckle grasp on the reins as Clove trotted down the lane, his mind racing. He cared for Grace more than anyone or anything else, and seeing her looking so tormented was enough to rattle him to his core. It also gave him a sinking feeling that she hadn't stopped when he'd called out to her. What could have possibly happened that caused her to behave so uncharacteristically?

When the buggy rounded a bend in the lane, passing the field of towering cornstalks that limited Aaron's vision, Grace finally came into view. Aaron expelled a long breath and blinked rapidly, forcing some moisture into his eyes. She'd gotten a significant lead on him while he was delayed with his horse, but he'd finally caught up with her. Soon he would be able to offer a shoulder to cry on and a soothing touch to wipe away her tears. He'd do whatever was possible to resolve the matter that had her upset, and he'd hold her until a smile returned to her face.

Grace peeked over her shoulder as the horse and buggy approached her, but she didn't halt. If Aaron wasn't mistaken, he thought she'd scowled at him, but that seemed absurd as it was completely unlike her.

"Hey," Aaron said as he tugged on the reins, slowing Clove's pace to a walk as the buggy rolled along beside Grace. "What happened?"

Refusing to look at him, Grace continued forward, fighting to catch her breath as her lower lip trembled. Though she was trim and fit, her emotional state and hurried pace had her sounding dreadfully winded.

"Grace, talk to me." Aaron peered out of the open side of the buggy, alarm bells ringing. Was…was she upset with *him*?

What felt like hours passed. Grace kept marching forward, remaining silent.

"Grace, *wass iss letz*?"

Still no response.

"You know," Aaron started, his hands shaking as he gripped the reins, his eyes having been off the road for quite some time, "we're a courting couple. I'm your beau. How are we supposed to have a relationship if we don't communicate?"

Grace let out a loud scoff as she stopped in her tracks.

She spun to face him, turquoise eyes blazing with fury. "I can assure you that we are no longer a courting couple, so maybe you should leave me alone."

Aaron's mouth dropped open. He tugged on the reins with such force that Clove issued an annoyed whinny. "W-what are you saying? What happened?"

"I think you, of all people, would know."

"I have no idea what you are talking about," Aaron answered, his response a bit louder and sharper than he'd intended.

Grace planted her hands on her hips. "I'm sorry," she replied, her voice dripping with sarcasm as she stepped up to the buggy. "Did you or did you not agree to get close to me because *Daadi* asked you to?"

Aaron's mouth went dry. *Annie,* he thought, groaning inwardly as he realized what had occurred. When his sister overheard his conversation with Eli earlier that afternoon, he'd briefly worried that she might spill the beans to someone, but he hadn't expected her to do it so soon. He'd planned to have a talk with her that night and ask her to keep what she'd heard to herself, but now it was too late.

"*Vell*? Nothing to say?"

Grace's shrill outburst startled both Aaron and his horse, both driver and beast flinching in unison.

"*Jah*, Eli did ask me to spend time with you, but he didn't tell me to—"

"You admit it!" Grace threw her hands in the air. "You never cared for me in the slightest! You pretended to be my friend, my beau, all so you could get your hands on the woodshop!"

She'd hit the nail on the head. True, Eli hadn't exactly demanded that Aaron befriend or court Grace to assume ownership of the business. But at the time, his confidence had been severely low, and he wasn't able to muster the courage to reject Eli's suggestion, especially after Eli had chosen him as his successor.

"That isn't exactly how it happened," he stated with conviction, though looking into Grace's weepy eyes caused his own to well up. "My intentions were *gut*. I would never knowingly hurt you."

Grace scoffed and looked up at the cloudless sky, the movement causing a torrent of tears to cascade down her flushed cheeks. "I'm not *schtupid*, Aaron. I told you how my first beau betrayed me by pretending to care for me, and you did the same thing, all while knowing how much that hurt me." She took a shuddering breath and wiped away her tears. "I trusted you and you broke that trust."

Aaron felt every ounce of air leave his lungs. Knowing that he was the cause of her immeasurable anguish was enough to make him sick.

"*Es dutt mer*," he apologized, clutching at his chest as his heart beat faster than the hooves of a galloping stallion.

"I don't care," Grace replied as she stared a hole right through him. "I don't ever want to see you again." Turning, she started forward without waiting for Aaron's reply.

This can't be happening. Aaron sat motionless in his buggy, sweating and shivering like he'd come down with a wicked summer flu. He now knew that Grace was furious with him, but he'd never expected her reaction of total rejection.

How could he fix this? How could he prove to her that he truly loved her?

He considered calling out to her that he was deeply, madly, head-over-heels in love with her but then nixed the idea. If she thought him to be a liar, she might find the sentiment tasteless. He thought about offering her a ride home but quickly discarded the idea. If she never wanted to lay eyes on him again, surely, she wouldn't want to sit close beside him in the buggy.

As Aaron took one last look at Grace's retreating form, becoming smaller and smaller as she hurried into the peaceful countryside, he felt anything but peaceful. He would never feel peace again. How could he, knowing that he'd lost the love of his life to an obscene misunderstanding, and maybe his own cowardness as well?

Feeling nearly sick to his stomach with an intense grief that he'd never felt before, Aaron let his head drop into his hands. He wept for what felt like an hour before picking the reins up, turning the horse in the middle of the road, and heading for home.

Chapter Fifteen

Grace held her breath as she slowly opened the cottage's back door and slipped inside. She tiptoed across the small house, hoping to remain unnoticed. She didn't feel like explaining the tear stains on her cheeks, and if Eli noticed, he would certainly ask. There was nothing she desired more than to be left alone with her shattered heart, knowing that no encouragement or platitudes would soothe her despair.

When she reached her quiet, small bedroom, she closed the door silently behind her. She let out a pent-up breath as she padded to her bed, then collapsed onto the quilt as a new wave of tears arrived. She rolled onto her side and hugged one of the pillows, unable to stop what seemed to be an endless flow of tears. Fearing that she might be heard weeping, she moved the pillow to her face and sobbed into it. Perhaps this sickening, embarrassing, horrid feeling was exactly what she deserved for believing that finding love, a true soulmate, was part of the Lord's plan for her life.

"Gracie? Are you home?"

She sat up and wiped away her tears with the sleeve of her dress. "*Jah, Daadi*. I'm in my room," she called back, trying to sound as nonchalant as possible.

"*Ach*, so early? I thought you wouldn't be home 'til suppertime." Eli's muffled voice grew louder as the thumping of his cane drew nearer.

"I'm feeling a little *grank* so I came home," she fibbed, straining to keep her voice from wavering. "You better stay out there so you don't catch whatever I have."

"Nonsense," Eli replied as Grace watched the brass doorknob turn. "If you're under the weather, you'll need some tending to." He entered the room, took one look at Grace through his thick glasses, and frowned. "*Wass iss letz*, Gracie?" He hurried over to her, his shuffling feet nearly becoming tangled in the braided area rug.

Upon seeing the compassion etched across her grandfather's wrinkled face, Grace turned back into a puddle of tears. "I'm sorry I lied, *Daadi*. I'm not really *grank*."

"Seems to me you're *grank* at heart, which could be just as serious as any illness." He took a seat on the bed beside her. "What's got you looking so blue?"

Grace looked away from him and fixed her gaze on the pastoral scene just beyond the nearby window. "*Ich lieb dich, Daadi*. I don't want to be disrespectful," she hiccupped on a sob, "but why did you ask Aaron to—"

"So that's what all these tears are about," Eli interrupted. He reached into his trousers pocket and pulled out a freshly laundered bandanna that he used as a handkerchief and handed it to his granddaughter. "There's nothin' that a *daadi* wants more than to see his *kinner* and *kinnskind* follow the Lord and be at peace. You've followed *Gott* since you were little, Gracie, but you haven't been at peace in quite some time."

Grace said nothing as she dabbed the handkerchief at the dampness on her cheeks. She knew she couldn't argue with Eli's observation.

"I've known Aaron since he was a *bu*," *Daadi* continued as he rested both hands on his cane's handle, "and I dare say that he's struggled to find peace as well, but for reasons different from yours. I hoped that two souls who were hurting might find comfort in each other."

Grace remained silent, unsure of how to respond. She loved her grandfather dearly and knew he would never intentionally do anything to hurt her, yet the pain she was experiencing was still very real and raw.

"I'm awful sorry that I caused you even the smallest amount of grief, Gracie. Truly, I am." He offered a pained, cautious grin. "Probably should've taken my own advice and talked to *Gott* about my concerns instead."

Grace chuckled on a sob. She couldn't stay upset with her dear *Daadi*. She placed her hand on top of his and gave it a tender pat. "I know, *Daadi*. *Ich lieb dich*." She removed her hand and used the handkerchief a second time to wipe her eyes. "It's really Aaron's fault. He could have declined your suggestion. He chose to pretend to…" She paused, choosing her words carefully. "He chose to pretend that he cared about me."

Eli's gray, bushy eyebrows climbed up his forehead. "Doesn't he?"

"Of course not. He saw his friendship with me as a favor for you, or as a requirement for him to take over the woodshop when you retire." Suddenly overcome with exhaustion, her posture slumped. "How could he possibly care for me when he only saw our friendship as a chore?"

"Sometimes love… I mean…friendship is like a seedling that was planted too early in springtime, but with a little warmth and patience, it blossoms and thrives for a lifetime." A serene smile decorated Eli's face as he stared into space, perhaps recalling fond memories of his beloved late wife.

Still feeling far too much heartache to take comfort in her grandfather's proverb, Grace said nothing.

"*Vell* now, how about we go sit on the porch and have a cold glass of blackberry lemonade? That always makes me feel better," Eli said as he stood and shuffled toward the door.

"*Nee denki*," Grace replied, feeling so heartsick that she couldn't imagine leaving the confines of the small bedroom. "I think I'll lie down for a few hours until it's time to fix supper."

"*Oll recht*, Gracie," Eli replied, seemingly understanding that she needed to be alone. "Have yourself a *gut* rest." He stepped out of the room and pulled the door shut behind him.

Grace stood and aimlessly wandered to the window. She stared outside, focusing on nothing in particular, still too numb to function. She sincerely appreciated the conversation she'd shared with her grandfather, and the wisdom that he'd given her, but it had done nothing to soothe her deep wounds. The afternoon sunlight that poured through the window warmed her skin, yet she felt cold.

Unwanted images of Aaron appeared in her mind's eye and she was brought to tears once again. A storm of clashing emotions whirled around inside her, swirling like a tornado and nearly just as destructive.

How will I ever recover from this? Grace longed for Aaron's nearness and the tender way that he held her hand, yet she knew she couldn't bear to be in the same room with him ever again. She would pine for the warmth that his chocolate eyes always held when he looked her way, yet how could she ever look him in the eye again after discovering that he'd tricked her into believing their intimate connection was genuine?

Crippled by a mixture of woe and fatigue, she turned to face her bed. However, the four steps it would take to reach the comfortable mattress seemed impossible. Melting into a whimpering mess, she lowered herself onto the floor, curled into a ball, and wept until there were no tears left.

"*Guder mariye*," Eli said over his shoulder as Aaron stepped into the woodshop on Monday morning.

What's good about it? Aaron asked himself, knowing he couldn't say the words out loud while remaining respectful. Instead, he muttered a melancholy "hello" while keeping his head down, too uncomfortable to risk the chance of their eyes meeting.

Aaron had been crawling out of his skin since Saturday afternoon, having been unable to eat or sleep since his spat with Grace. The deeply disturbing restlessness that he now carried threatened to drive him mad, and being on Ebersol property wasn't soothing that stress away. On top of losing the woman he loved, he was certainly about to lose his job as well. It would only be a matter of time until Eli found out that he'd demolished Grace's heart, if he wasn't aware of that fact already. What grandfather would allow the man who emotionally devastated his granddaughter to continue to work for him, let alone inherit his business?

It doesn't matter, Aaron thought as he took off his straw hat and hung it on his designated wall peg. If he didn't have Grace, he didn't have anything. He no longer cared about his job, since it would not bring him any joy. He no longer cared about inheriting Ebersol's Country Furniture, since there was no future for him without Grace. He would simply exist in a state of numbness until the Lord called him home.

"Are you *oll recht*?"

Aaron lifted his head at Eli's question, but didn't turn to face him. "I guess I'm just wondering if I should head home or if you would permit me to work until you can hire my replacement."

Eli, who'd been preoccupied with sorting through several order slips at a metal shop desk, slowly spun around in his chair and gawked at Aaron with a deeply puzzled expression. "What in the world are you talking about?"

Aaron ignored the burning sensation in his face as he glanced out the nearby open window, wishing that he might jump out and run far away. "Grace and I...we aren't...we—"

Eli held up his calloused hand. "I heard about that, but it doesn't mean that you aren't needed here."

"But—"

"But nothing," Eli interjected, waving his hand through the air. "You're a *wunderbaar gut* craftsman, and you've proven to me that you have what it takes to become my business's new owner. You aren't backing out on our agreement, are you?"

Still unable to look at Eli, Aaron fiddled with his suspenders. "I don't want to back out, but I don't think Grace will like seeing me around here." He heard the catch in his voice and bit down hard on his tongue to keep himself from breaking down. Straightening his posture, he finally allowed himself to make eye contact with his employer, a man whom he had considered one of his only friends for the longest time. "I want to do what is best for Grace."

Eli gave a lopsided grin, though his concern was carved more deeply across his face than his wrinkles. "*Kumme* and sit over here with me. I think we need to have ourselves a talk."

Aaron slogged across the woodshop, not terribly keen on conversing at that moment. He didn't feel any relief in learning that his job was safe, nor was he thrilled that ownership of the business would soon be passed to him. The only thing he wanted, to hold and cherish Grace, was permanently out of his reach. He doubted he'd find comfort in anything ever again.

Once Aaron was seated on the old stool that was adjacent to Eli's desk, he glanced down and noticed scatterings of sawdust beneath his worn work boots. "I didn't do a *gut* job of sweeping in here on Friday night."

"I ain't the least bit worried about that," Eli said, his solemn gaze fixed intently on his young employee. "I'm more concerned about the apology I owe you, and it's time I finally say it."

"Apology?"

"*Jah*." Eli removed his glasses, pulled a handkerchief out of his pocket, and cleaned the lenses. "I'm sorry if I made you feel pressured to pursue my Gracie." Once his glasses were back in place, the sincere remorse in his eyes was greatly magnified. "I thought you both might find comfort in each other, and I hoped...*vell*, I hoped that things might've turned out differently. It was a *narrish* of me to have interfered with your lives."

"*Nee*, it wasn't *narrish* at all," Aaron vehemently protested, leaning forward in his seat. "Courage has never been my strong suit, and if you hadn't given me a push, I would have never gotten to know Grace." A pained smile crossed his lips. "It was a blessing, even if it was short-lived."

Eli's face brightened at that, and the deeply etched wrinkles on his face seemed to soften. "It's none of my business, 'specially at this point, but you really do *lieb* Gracie, don't you?"

Aaron didn't hesitate. The words slipped out as naturally as the sun rose each morning. "*Jah*, I do. I love Grace with all of my heart." He dropped his gaze for just a moment, nearly overcome with emotion. He quickly collected himself and raised his head, his eyes locking with Eli's. "She…she somehow saw into my soul and fixed me."

"*Vell*," Eli said as he stroked his wiry beard, "only *Gott* can truly fix what ails a person." He paused, reached for a nearby thermos, and took a long drink from it. "You know how certain crops are planted side by side since they can help each other to grow?"

Aaron hesitated, feeling a sense of whiplash. "*Jah*, sure. But what does that have to do with Grace and me?"

"Just like farmers and gardeners place certain plants together, our Heavenly Father does the same with his children. More often than not, He'll place someone in your life to help you grow. It sounds like *Gott* planted you and Gracie in the same *gaarde*."

Though he was touched by Eli's wise insight, emotional agony still tormented Aaron like a horsefly that couldn't be shooed away. "*Jah*, but none of it matters now. I never got the chance to tell her how much I care for her." He let his head fall into his hands and shivered despite the balminess of the woodshop. "She'll never know since she won't allow me to speak with her."

They sat in silence for quite some time before Aaron

lifted his head. He stared pleadingly at Eli, desperate for any suggestion of what might ease his suffering.

Eli looked right back at him, tight-lipped and stone-faced.

When Aaron could no longer take it, he finally asked, "What should I do?"

"I'm not too keen on putting my two cents in, considering what happened." Eli's gaze trailed off toward a newly crafted hope chest that needed to be sanded and stained, just one project on a mile-long list.

"*Nee*, I'm asking for your help," Aaron persisted. He faked a cough in hopes of suppressing the tears that threatened to wash him away. "Please."

Eli leaned back. Both he and the ancient wooden chair that he was seated on let out a groan. "I can tell you what I would do if I was in your shoes, but it's up to you to decide which path to take."

Aaron nodded.

"If you truly *lieb* Gracie, if you believe she's the woman that *Gott* has intended to be your partner, you can't let her go without a fight. You'll need to prove to her, beyond a shadow of a doubt, that your *lieb* is sincere."

"How should I do that?"

Eli turned his palms upward. "I don't know, but I do know that if you pray about it, you'll eventually be given an answer."

The sound of a car engine and tires crunching against the gravel driveway drifted in through the open window.

"A customer," Eli said as he rose slowly with a grunt. "I'll go see how I can help them." He reached for his cane. "Maybe you'll want to use this time to have a talk with *Gott*."

Aaron watched Eli disappear into the adjacent show-room and allowed his mind to marinate on everything Eli had said.

He did have a point, Aaron thought, staring once again at the sawdust on the floor. Grace's trust in him was de-stroyed, and if he had any chance at winning her back, he needed to prove his love to her. But how in the world could he do that?

At a loss, Aaron removed his straw hat, closed his eyes, and folded his hands in his lap. It was time to talk to the Lord.

Chapter Sixteen

The rest of the week dragged on as Aaron showed up for work every day, longing for a moment alone with Grace, yet unsure of what he'd say if he was granted his wish. He'd seen her only a few times in passing, when she was hanging laundry on the clothesline and when she brought Eli's lunch out to the woodshop. They still hadn't exchanged a single word, and he'd been downright shocked to see that she'd prepared a light meal for him as well.

"Aren't you going to eat?" Eli had asked the first time the phenomenon had occurred.

"I brought a sack lunch from home," Aaron replied, still stunned by Grace's gesture. "I didn't think Grace would—"

"She may be out of sorts, but she wouldn't think of letting anyone go hungry," Eli interrupted before taking a bite of his egg salad sandwich.

So, Aaron ate both lunches, not wanting what he'd brought from home to go to waste and also desperate to avoid offending Grace more than he already had. Not expecting her to continue providing his meal, he brought a lunch with him each day that week. To his continued surprise, Grace still provided a noon meal for him each day. If he wasn't so consumed with concern regarding the state of their relationship, he would have found the situation nearly humorous, though he quickly grew tired of over-eating and then heading back to physical labor.

A local bookstore owner showed up at about ten o'clock on Friday morning and inquired about having some new bookshelves made. The new customer, a Mennonite and good friend of Eli's, had also offered to drive him into town and treat him to lunch at the Bird-in-Hand Family Restaurant. Never one to turn down a hearty meal, Eli readily agreed, leaving Aaron alone in the woodshop.

As he brushed a coat of golden stain across the hope chest that was scheduled to be picked up on Monday, Aaron found himself glancing out the shop's back door that had been propped open. He had a clear view of Grace as she picked the last of the vegetables from the little garden near the cottage, her face far too lovely to look so terribly solemn.

Was now the right time to reach out to her? Aaron glanced around the lonely woodshop. Eli's faithful presence was noticeably absent, and unless a customer visited the business, he and Grace would have plenty of time to talk privately.

He glanced back toward the garden, still pondering if he should take action, and immediately froze when he locked eyes with Grace. The icy look she gave him was frigid enough to instantly freeze Mill Creek. Cringing, Aaron spun around and scurried into the showroom, needing some privacy to recover. Though he was well aware that Grace's perception of him was no longer favorable, he'd clung to a thread of hope that her burning animosity toward him would lessen with each day that passed. Clearly, that wasn't the case.

His stomach rapidly turned sour from his emotional turmoil as he paced around the showroom. What would he do if he couldn't win Grace back? He couldn't imagine living the rest of his life without the sweetness of her laughter, her eagerness to encourage others, and the way a single glance in her direction could take his breath away. A life without Grace wasn't worth living, and Aaron wasn't looking forward to spending the rest of his years on Earth wallowing in downright misery.

The phone in the woodshop, which their district's bishop allowed for business purposes, suddenly rang, interrupting Aaron's lament. He heaved a sigh and dragged himself across the showroom toward the woodshop, completely zapped of energy.

He'd just passed through the door that connected the showroom to the woodshop when Grace suddenly burst in. Neither of them said a single word as they gawked at each other, while the phone continued to ring.

"Are you going to get that?" Grace spat her question at him, her hands firmly mounted on her hips.

For a moment, Aaron almost danced with joy, though he'd never danced a day in his life before. His love had finally spoken to him after nearly a week of silence, though her words certainly weren't those of endearment.

"I was just about to," Aaron replied as he stuck his thumb out and then gestured over his shoulder. "I was—"

"I'll get it," Grace interrupted him as she marched across the spacious room, her nose in the air. She picked up the phone and held the receiver to her ear, purposefully turning her back to Aaron. "Ebersol's Country Furniture, this is Grace." There was a brief pause. "Oh, hi, *Daed. Wie ghets*?" Another pause. "*Ach*, really? I thought we wouldn't need to pack up the cottage for another two or three weeks."

She turned ever so slightly, peeking at Aaron out of the corner of her eye. The displeasure on her face softened into something that Aaron couldn't quite identify. Was that disappointment, relief, or perhaps a strange concoction of the two?

"*Jah*, we can be ready to go by then. I'll let *Daadi* know as soon as he gets back from town," she said, turning her back to Aaron once again. She nibbled on her fingernails as she listened to the caller. "Okay, *Daed*, we'll see you soon. *Mach gute*." She placed the phone back on its receiver and then stared at it, almost as if lost in a haze of disbelief.

"It…it sounds like you're heading back to Paradise," Aaron said quietly as Grace hurried past without giving him a second glance.

"*Jah*, and Eli too," she shot back over her shoulder without slowing her stride. "I suspect that's nothing you'll cry about."

"What? Why would you think that?"

Grace spun around with the speed and fury of a tornado. "*Daadi* will soon be retired, then this place will be all yours and we'll be out of your hair." She scoffed as she gestured widely around the room. "Just what you always wanted, *jah*?"

Aaron frowned so severely that his face ached. Her words pierced him like a pitchfork carelessly tossed into a pile of hay. "Do you truly believe that I care more about the business than you and Eli?"

Grace's scowl slowly faded as her eyes grew shiny. Her face became flushed, though the ruddiness in her cheeks seemed to stem more from pain than anger. "I was *nar-*

rish enough to fall in *lieb* with the man I was tricked into courting and can never trust again. So, honestly, I don't know what to think." A single tear escaped from her left eye and she erased it with a quick brush of her fingers. "So, enjoy this business, Aaron. You certainly earned it." Several more tears rolled down her cheeks and splashed onto her mauve chore dress. With that, she hitched up the hem of her dress and dashed out of the woodshop.

Aaron watched helplessly as Grace fled, his feet feeling as if they were cemented to the floor. The sight of her weeping shook him to his core, yet what could he do, what could he say to comfort her? She still saw him as the enemy and would undoubtedly disregard anything that he might share with her.

She said she loves me. It hit him like a stack of bricks that Grace's tearful declaration of love for him had also been her first. Oh, what he would have given to boldly proclaim his love for her, gather her into his arms, and share their first kiss. But that was out of the question now, and she'd probably assume his confession of love was nothing more than a ploy to manipulate her.

Knowing that only the Lord could help him, Aaron lowered himself onto his knees, closed his eyes, held his palms upward, and prayed out loud. "Father in Heaven, you already know that I love Grace with all of my heart, and that an awful misunderstanding has come between us. I ask that you put it on her heart to consider who I truly am. If it is your will, I ask that you'll bring us together once more. Grant me the patience of Job, the wisdom of Solomon, and the compassion of your Son so that I may carry on with my life. In Jesus's name, I pray. Amen."

Though a deep melancholy still lingered in his chest,

Aaron felt a sense of peace after talking with his Creator. He moseyed back to the hope chest, picked up his brush, and resumed the process of staining the piece, knowing that even without his Grace, the grace of the Lord would sustain him.

Grace was stunned when her father phoned around noon that Friday to tell her that he and several other members of her immediate family would be coming to move Eli's belongings out of the cottage. With the construction of the *daadi haus* completed, her time here in Bird-in-Hand had come to an end. Frankly, she didn't know how to feel about returning to her family's farm in Paradise. Sure, she looked forward to reconnecting with her loved ones and settling back into her own familiar bedroom, yet she couldn't help but feel that a piece of her heart would always be here in Bird-in-Hand. She'd come to love the little village, the homey cottage, the rolling hills, and the people she'd met, especially one person in particular.

"*Ach*, I've never been more *verhuddelt*," Grace muttered to herself as she gently hoisted a box that contained some dinnerware and silverware. Aaron King had certainly turned her world upside-down. The intense love her heart sang for him clashed with the devastation she'd experienced when she realized that the deep fondness she'd assumed they'd shared was certainly not mutual. A part of her never wanted to see Aaron again in hopes that her grief over their breakup would lessen, but at the same time, she couldn't imagine living happily without gazing into the eyes of the man she loved above all others.

Grace moved toward the door but stopped before she reached it. She turned and glanced around the small kitchen, now empty like the rest of the little house. She and Eli had stayed up late Friday night and worked all day Saturday, neatly packing the contents of the house into large cardboard boxes. Like most members of their community, Eli and his late wife lived a simple, humble lifestyle, so preparing everything to move wasn't an overwhelming task. Now, on Monday morning, only the furniture remained indoors, which her father, brothers, and brother-in-law would move out.

A breeze of nostalgia swept through Grace as she surveyed her surroundings. Even though the summer had ended on a bitterly sour note, she knew she'd always look back on her time spent in Bird-in-Hand with deep affection. The weeks spent having one-on-one conversations with *Daadi*, gleaning his wisdom, and whispering sweet-nothings with Aaron were nothing more than memories now.

There'd been a time, not so long ago, when she'd daydreamed about the possibility of marrying Aaron and starting their life together in this very cottage, as happy newlyweds. When they were blessed with children, they could add onto the cottage so there was room enough for a large family. She'd pictured herself and Aaron with wrinkled faces and white hair, sitting on the porch, watching the stars, and reminiscing about their many joyful years together.

There was no chance of that now. Grace willed herself not to shed another tear over her heartbreak, at least for today. Soon her family would arrive with several spring wagons to transport Eli, his belongings, and herself back to Paradise. Plastering on a brave face, Grace took a deep breath and pushed the screen door open with her backside.

It was time to say goodbye to the cottage, to Bird-in-Hand, and to her hopes of living her very own happily ever after.

She made her way across the lawn and set down the box she'd been carrying among the other boxes that she carried outside earlier that morning. None of the boxes had been too heavy for her to handle, and even if they were, she would have insisted that Eli not lift a finger. Her parents and some of her siblings would arrive any moment, and there would be plenty of hands to pitch in.

"*Wie ghets*, Grace?"

She spun around, spooked by the male voice. "*Ach*, you scared the wits outta me, Aaron!" She swiped away some beads of sweat from her forehead. "What do you want?"

Aaron, who'd called to her from across the yard, stopped in his tracks, his mouth twisted into a grimace. "Sorry." He took a single step forward, clearly hesitant to approach her. His hands slid into his trousers pockets. "You and Eli are leaving today, *jah*? I just wanted to wish you safe travels."

"*Denki*," Grace replied bluntly, willing herself not to cry at the sight of him. The ever-constant battle within her raged on, the deep grief he'd caused her forcing her to look away from him, yet her unyielding love making it so she couldn't look away.

They stood far apart in awkward silence for several moments until the melody of an army of horseshoes clip-clopping against asphalt sounded in the distance. A wagon appeared over the crest of the hill that was immediately followed by two others.

"My *familye* is about to arrive," Grace stated as she made her way across the lawn, heading for the driveway. "*Mache gut*."

"*Jah*, you too," Aaron muttered as she passed him.

Grace inhaled the scent of the woodshop, which clung heavily to Aaron, a familiar scent that she'd once found comforting. Pretending as if the deep longing to embrace him wasn't clawing at her spirit, she continued forward, until she heard footsteps behind her. Was he following her?

Grace turned and frowned when she saw Aaron make a beeline toward the cottage. "What are you doing?" she called to him as she placed her hand on her brow, shielding her eyes from the sun.

"I need to have a word with Eli," Aaron replied over his shoulder as he neared the front door.

"He's napping on the couch. Best let him be," Grace huffed, irritated with the clomping of his work boots on the porch's wooden floor.

Aaron glanced toward the lane and then back at Grace. "*Vell*, he's gonna have to get up anyway since your folks are here to load everything up. I'll do my best not to startle him."

Grace's frustration bubbled over. "You may own the business now, but the *haus* isn't yours. I don't know who you think you are, but you can't just—"

Aaron's face suddenly blanched. "I know who I am, Grace. I think it's *you* who doesn't understand who I truly am." With that, he placed his hand on the doorknob and let himself into the cottage.

Grace groaned and threw her hands in the air as a sudden wave of exhaustion swept over her. Aaron had never spoken so directly to her, which had taken her aback. Maybe he was right. Maybe he wasn't the soft-spoken, timid man that she'd fallen in love with. Figuring out Aaron

King felt more challenging than trying to bake an apple pie without any apples.

Yet there was one thing that she was certain of; she couldn't continue living her life like this. She'd struggled for the longest time after her first beau's betrayal. Now, her breakup with Aaron, whom she loved more than anyone else, had nearly done her in. It was time for a change.

Instead of rushing to the driveway to meet the first wagon that had pulled in, Grace reached out to her Heavenly Father, deciding to finally give Him all of the pieces of her broken heart.

Lord, for the longest time I've carried the burden of pain; pain over losing my first beau, and now pain caused by losing Aaron. Though I'll struggle to ignore my longings to spend the rest of my days at his side, I know that if I hand you the reins of my life, you'll guide me to peace. I want to trust in you fully and I ask that you help me surrender fully to your will. Amen.

Grace opened her eyes and lifted her head. She suddenly felt lighter than she had since she was a young girl. Yes, she still loved Aaron and would spend the rest of her life wondering what would have happened if their relationship had continued, but the persistent ache in her spirit was noticeably absent, and she knew that the prayer she'd whispered in her heart had been heard.

She took in a deep breath of fresh country air, sweetened by the earthy odors of fresh-cut hay and the arrival of cooler autumn temperatures. Grace turned once again and rushed to meet her family as their wagons turned into the driveway, knowing that she'd fully given her heart to the only one who would never break it.

Chapter Seventeen

Grace's father, Jacob, and her mother, Leona, arrived in the first wagon, both of them shouting and waving their greetings. They brought the small wagon to a halt near the small stable, jumped down from their seat, and scurried over to Grace.

Leona took Grace in her ample arms, gushing over how *wunderbaar gut* it was to see her daughter again.

Jacob waited for his turn to embrace their youngest child but soon issued a mock grumble. "You'd think Grace was gone for a whole year with the way you're carrying on, and she's been less than ten miles away this whole time."

Leona wiped a joyful tear from her eyes, the same lovely turquoise color that she'd passed along to each of her children. "It felt like one hundred years and one hundred miles." She took both of her daughter's hands in her own. "Tell us, how was your summer with your *daadi*? Is he doing well?"

Before Grace could answer, a second team of huge draft horses pulled a wagon into the drive. Her eldest sibling, broad-shouldered Jesse, was at the reins and guided his team up to the stable. Fun-loving, lanky Elias, another of her elder brothers, rode in the bed of the wagon, comically bouncing around as the rig jostled along. A third small wagon immediately followed the second, bringing Grace's dearest sister, short and stout Abby, and her husband, tall and lean Paul.

The very lively reunion increased in volume and excitement as everyone chatted. Grace enjoyed bantering with everyone who'd come to lend a hand, though she couldn't help but notice Abby casting furtive glances in her direction, her eyes brimming with curiosity. Surely, the sibling that Grace was closest to could sense that something was amiss.

Much to Grace's relief, her sister didn't have time to ask any questions.

"Now that we're all here, let's not waste any time," their father spoke up, his strong voice ringing out above the others. "Is everything ready to go, Grace?"

Grace bobbed her head and pointed to the cluster of moving boxes that she'd piled near the cottage. "Everything is all packed up, except for the furniture."

"No matter, we won't have enough room in the wagons for everything today," Jacob replied enthusiastically. "If you women don't mind loading the lighter boxes into the first wagon, us menfolk will load the heavier boxes into the second wagon. Then, us men can load what furniture we can fit into wagon number three. We'll just come back tomorrow for whatever furniture we have to leave behind today."

"There'd be more space in the wagon if Elias didn't insist on riding in the back like a little *boppli*," Jesse commented to no one in particular as the group headed for the cottage.

"Puh!" Elias gave Jesse a lighthearted shove, his feigned annoyance poorly hidden behind a mischievous grin. "Call me a *boppli* all you want, but being hunkered down in the wagon bed is the safest place to be when you are at the reins."

Everyone but Grace chuckled at that.

Just as they neared the cottage, the screen door swung open, capturing everyone's attention. Eli emerged through the door, his wrinkles appearing suddenly deeper as a distinct frown crossed his thin lips. Aaron, looking equally as ruffled, followed Eli down the creaking porch steps, then scooted around him and slunk toward the stable.

How odd, Grace mused as she watched Aaron tiptoe away, slightly hunched over as if a violent gust of wind was blowing against him. He looked even more timid than usual. Had he and Eli had some sort of argument?

"*Ach*, it's so good to see you, *Daed*," Jacob gushed, flitting over to his elderly father with childlike energy. "We've been waiting for this day for such a long time! It'll be *wunderbaar gut* to have you living in Paradise with us!"

Eli offered his son a pained grin. "I've also been looking forward to that, but I'm afraid we're going to have to wait a little while longer."

"What do you mean?" Jacob asked as he stared at his father in disbelief.

"Looks like all your stuff is packed up and ready to go," Leona chimed in, tilting her head to the side. "What's stopping you from moving into the new *daadi haus*?"

Eli let out a long sigh. With great effort and carefulness, he lowered himself onto the top porch step. When he was seated, he sighed again. "The *yung* man who was going to become the new owner of Ebersol's Country Furniture, as of today, just backed out of our deal."

Grace let out a gasp that sounded more like a shriek, causing several of her family members to flinch.

"Not only that," Eli went on as he took off his straw hat and used it to fan his face, "he also resigned from his carpentry position."

Everyone exchanged bewildered glances.

"It's a real pity too," Eli said to no one in particular as he stared down at the pink petunias that Grace had planted on both sides of the stairs shortly after her arrival in Bird-in-Hand. "He was the perfect man for the job."

Grace was flabbergasted. The shocking news caused her to feel nearly lightheaded, her vision swirling as she tried to process what she'd just heard. What in the world could have happened to cause Aaron to give up the business he so desperately wanted to call his own? Even if he changed his mind about owning the business, it seemed absurd for him to forfeit a job that he found great satisfaction in. Was he upset with her and taking his frustration out on Eli? Was he having some sort of breakdown?

Grace swayed unsteadily, feeling suddenly frantic. She blinked several times and steadied herself, then looked toward the stable. Aaron was hitching his horse to his buggy, his back turned to the Ebersol clan. She couldn't let him leave without an explanation.

"Aaron," she called to him as she took a few shaky steps forward, the grassy ground feeling like quicksand beneath her feet. "*Kumme* here, please!"

She held her breath as he made his way to her, the seconds passing like centuries as he walked over from the barn. He kept his eyes trained on the path in front of him, the brim of his straw hat hiding his face.

When he reached the now confused group of Ebersols,

Aaron said nothing. He finally raised his head, his eyes nervously taking in the small crowd that congregated behind Grace before finally focusing on her.

Suddenly aware of the whispers behind her, Grace forced her attention back to Aaron. "What are you...why did—"

"I had to walk away," Aaron interrupted her, his broad shoulders lifting in a sad shrug.

Grace swallowed against the lump in her throat. "Why? How could you put my *daadi* in this position?"

Aaron glanced around at the faces that were staring at him, some of them wearing looks of shock and others unable to hide their confusion. His face reddened as he answered her question. "I'd never want to leave Eli in the lurch, but it's not right for me to take over the business if you think I took advantage of our friendship to gain it." He peeked over at her family before lifting his chin. "I love you, Grace, and I couldn't let you think that."

Grace gasped as her hand flew to her chest. *He loves me?*

Aaron stole another glimpse at Grace's collectively stunned family then returned his attention to her. His mouth contorted into an awkward grin. "Besides, running a business that is linked to you while having to let you go at the same time would be impossible, so it's best that I go to work on my *daed*'s dairy farm instead."

Unshed tears burned in Grace's eyes. Aaron loved her enough to walk away from the chance to own a very well-established, successful business. He loved her enough to walk away from the only career path that he'd ever known. He loved her enough to throw his future into uncertainty. On top of that, he loved her enough to boldly proclaim his love for her. It was a rather vulnerable action to take, especially in front of a group of people who were strangers to him. Knowing Aaron as well as she did, Grace was certain that the transparency he'd publicly displayed had undoubtedly been difficult to muster.

Two selfless acts that prove he loves me.

Aaron gave a very weak smile before turning away to return to his waiting horse and buggy.

"Wait," Grace blurted, startled by the volume of her voice.

He turned to look at her, his eyebrows quizzically raised.

Suddenly very aware of all the pairs of eyes on her, Grace felt like she was an *Englisch* actress on a stage with a blinding spotlight shining on her. "Let's go inside so we can talk," she said just above a whisper.

Trusting that Aaron would follow her, Grace buzzed like a hummingbird toward the cottage, bounded up the stairs where her widely grinning grandfather was still seated, and slipped into the privacy of the little house.

"Please close the door behind you," Grace said to Aaron the moment his work boots landed on the kitchen's linoleum floor. "I think we put on enough of a show for one day, *jah*?"

"Sure, of course." Aaron closed both the screen door and the heavier oak one after it, surprised by the lightness in Grace's tone. Initially, she'd seemed shocked, if not downright offended, by his decision to walk away from the business that was promised to him. Truthfully, the idea to forfeit his chance to own the business of his dreams had shaken him deeply and had also been the cause of several sleepless nights. However, after much soul-searching and a heart-to-heart talk with the Lord, Aaron knew he'd made the right decision, painful as it was. If his stepping out of the picture would give Grace even an ounce of peace, then it would be worth it.

He snuck a peek out the nearby window and caught a glimpse of Eli chatting with his adult children and grandchildren, all of whom were wearing smiles, but none shined as brightly as Eli's. That puzzled Aaron, given that not even ten minutes ago the old man had been deeply sullen at his abrupt departure from their business agreement. Was it possible that Eli was secretly glad to be free of him, just as Grace surely was?

Ultimately, it didn't matter what opinions anyone harbored about him. For the first time in his life, Aaron had finally revealed his true feelings, and the unfamiliar sense of peace was nearly as warm and sweet as a blueberry pie fresh out of the oven.

"Could you *kumme* sit with me, please?"

Grace's meek request brought his attention back to the current moment. "*Jah*, sure." He moved toward the small, circular table and wondered what his former sweetheart wanted to discuss privately. Was she going to chew him out for delaying Eli's move to Paradise? Maybe she was going to scold him for embarrassing her in front of her family.

Aaron seated himself across from Grace and waited for her to say something. What felt like minutes ticked by as the silence between them lingered, yet he didn't want to push her into sharing what was on her mind. He studied her as she stared down at her hands that were folded in her lap, her lips pressed tightly together and her face serious. Even looking so thoughtful, she was the loveliest woman that the Lord had ever created, both in face and spirit, and he wanted to memorize everything about her in this moment, which would likely be their last conversation ever.

The silence between them continued, causing Aaron to become antsy. "Grace, I know you don't trust me and I'm sorry that—"

Grace finally looked up and her tear-filled eyes locked on his. "When I was a little *maedel*," she started, interrupting him, "I spent a lot of time daydreaming about my future, especially wondering if there would be a special man in my life." She reached up and brushed away a tear before it could roll down her sun-kissed cheek. "I wondered if he'd be silly and outgoing or serious and thoughtful. I wondered if he'd be a dairyman or a blacksmith or a builder. I wondered how many *kinner* we might have someday."

Aaron sat on the edge of his seat, fighting the urge to rush over to Grace and kiss away her tears. Oh, how deeply it pained him to see her weep, but knowing that there was nothing he could do to soothe her pained him even more.

"But none of that was really important," Grace continued after a shaky breath. "What matters most, what I've dreamed about my entire life, is falling for a man who would fearlessly, selflessly tell the world how much he loved me."

She reached for his hand and firmly grasped it, her gentle touch familiar yet new and exciting at the same time.

"That man is you, Aaron. You're the man I've dreamed of for my whole life."

Aaron blinked several times, nearly in disbelief at what he was hearing, though one look at the way that Grace beamed at him through her joyful tears proved to him that she was sincere.

"*Ich lieb dich*, Grace," Aaron confessed, overwhelmed by the emotional intensity of the moment. "I really do."

"I know," Grace replied, her face nearly glowing with happiness. "I love you too."

Unable to contain his great joy, Aaron sprung up from his chair, knocking it over in the process. Grace giggled through her tears as he rushed over to her, scooped her up, and twirled her around in circles, relishing the closeness of her.

Aaron cradled Grace's face in his hands after setting her down on her feet. He gazed into her sparkling eyes, taken by the adoring way that she looked up at him. Finally free from self-doubt, he was granted his wish of kissing away the tears that watered the freckles on her face.

"Marry me, Grace," he whispered against her cheek, holding her so closely that he could practically feel her heartbeat. "Let me be your *mann*."

Grace nodded, her smile bright enough to light up all of Bird-in-Hand on the darkest night. "There's nothing I'd rather do than be your *fraa*."

That was all he needed to hear. They shared a kiss, and for the first time in his life, Aaron felt like he was right where he belonged.

When their lips parted, Grace rested her cheek against his chest. "*Denki* for making my dreams come true, Aaron. You mean the world to me."

Aaron planted a soft kiss on the top of her head. "Maybe it isn't me whom you should thank."

She looked up at him, still wrapped in his embrace. "Oh?"

"I was never comfortable in my own skin until I finally sought out the Lord's will. Once I accepted that He was in control, He blessed me with a little Grace."

She giggled at his pun and the melody of her laughter lifted him up to the clouds.

"*Kumme*," Grace said as she grasped his hand. "Let's go share our *gut* news with my *familye*."

As Aaron followed Grace to the door, his fingers intertwined with hers, a deep sense of peace overwhelmed him. The self-doubt that had stalked him since his youth would never again pose a threat to his happiness. With the Lord and Grace by his side, nothing again would ever hold him back.

Epilogue

On a snowy mid-December morning, Grace sat at the kitchen table writing out some Christmas cards. After addressing an envelope to her grandfather, she glanced around the small yet tidy kitchen, still fighting a sense of disbelief that this space was her very own.

She stood and wandered over to the window, squinting past the plump snowflakes to get a better view of the woodshop, where her new husband and his two recently hired employees were hard at work. Her thoughts drifted back to their wedding day, which had taken place on the second Thursday in November. After the wedding meal, Eli presented her and Aaron with a tiny wooden house that he had whittled as a tangible symbol of his wedding gift to them.

"It's time that the cottage be filled with a new generation of love," he'd declared as he placed the miniature wooden house in Grace's palm. Then, looking up at Aaron, Eli gave a little chuckle. "As long as the man of the house doesn't mind having such a long walk to work every day."

Grace grinned at the cherished memory and then imagined the lovely Christmas dinner she would soon host in this very room for her and Aaron's families. True, they would need to bring in some extra tables and chairs, and the tiny house would certainly be packed with so many people milling about, but knowing that the cottage would be filled to the brim with their loved ones brought Grace a deep sense of contentment.

She glanced at the braided area rug in the middle of the kitchen floor, where Amber, their newly-adopted feline, was curled up in a ball and purring like the engine of a tractor. Amber had been Annie's wedding gift to the couple, and the orange kitten brought much entertainment and laughter into the cottage.

The door suddenly swung open and Aaron burst into the cozy kitchen. A blast of icy air and several snowflakes floated in as he lunged to close the door behind him, fighting the arctic-like wind.

Grace chuckled, wondering if her new husband was putting on a show for her amusement. He'd become more animated and lighthearted since the day of their engagement, and it did her heart good to see him blossom like a late-blooming flower.

"Looks like we're going to have a white *Grischtdaag* this year," Aaron said, though his voice was muffled by the navy woolen scarf that was wrapped all the way from his neck up to his nose.

Grace bobbed her head as she took another look out the window. "I sure hope so. Something about having a blanket of snow on the ground makes Christmastime extra special, *jah*?"

"Agreed," Aaron replied as he took a spiral-bound notebook from beneath his arm and placed it on the table, then shed his scarf, coat, and black felt hat.

Grace glanced at the battery-operated clock that hung above the door. "Did you come in for lunch? You know

I would've brought something out for you and your new workers."

"You take such *gut* care of everyone, *mei lieb*, but I actually had an idea that I was so *eckseidt* about that I couldn't wait to tell you." He beamed as he sank into one of the dining chairs and opened the notebook. "*Kumme* look at this."

Grace seated herself across from Aaron, eager to see what he had to show her. She pushed the box of Christmas cards to the side and then took the notebook from her husband.

A large rectangle was drawn on the page. In the center of the rectangle were large letters that spelled out "Grace's Country Furniture." Several notes had been scribbled on the page's margin indicating that the sign would be made out of cherry or oak wood and hung with an iron rod above the customer's entrance to the showroom.

"What do you think?" Aaron asked, biting on his lower lip to suppress a premature grin.

Grace's eyebrows rose high on her forehead. Though she was the granddaughter of the woodshop's founder and the bride of the man who now called it his own, she truly had nothing to do with its everyday operations.

After she got through her initial bout of confusion, Grace finally found her voice. "You want to name the business after me? Is that what this means?"

"*Jah*, if it would be *oll recht* with you," Aaron answered as he scooted his chair closer to his wife.

Grace glanced down at the notebook and then back at Aaron, feeling thoroughly puzzled. "Of course, I'm honored by this, but why not call it Aaron's or King's Country Furniture? I don't have anything to do with the business, other than bringing your lunch out to you."

Aaron reached for one of her hands, brought it to his lips, and kissed it. "When I'm out working and can't spend time with you, I want constant reminders of the two things that mean most to me; the grace of *Gott*, and the Grace that I call my own."

"*Ach*, if that isn't the dearest thing I've ever heard," Grace exclaimed and she swiped away a joyful tear. She leaned over to kiss her husband, giggling when his short beard, a new symbol of their marriage, tickled her face.

"*Vell*, I better get back to work," Aaron declared as he rose and donned his coat. "We're a little ahead of schedule with our current orders, so maybe I'll have some time this afternoon to start work on the new sign." He placed his hat back on his head then wrapped the scarf around his neck and mouth as he made his way to the door. "*Ich lieb dich, fraa.*" With that loving sentiment, he tipped his face down, allowing the brim of his hat to take the brunt of the frigid wind as he stepped outside and then quickly pulled the door shut behind him.

Grace sighed contentedly as she returned to the window, watching her beloved Aaron as he tromped through the snow drifts that were now shin-high. She'd always hoped for her very own happily ever after, and the Lord had proven to her that His will for her life was even more fulfilling than her wildest dreams.

* * * * *

Dear Reader,

It can be difficult for me not to inject some of my personality traits into the characters that I create. Out of all the characters that appear in this story, I relate to Aaron most of all. As I was writing this very introverted character, I started seeing more and more of myself in his self-doubt and anxiety.

There was a point in the story when Aaron had to "let go and let God." That can be a difficult, and seemingly impossible, thing to do. Several years ago, I had my own such moment. At the time, I was suffering emotionally in a way that I never had experienced before. "Letting go and letting God" requires us to give up our own will so that we may completely surrender to Him, and doing so was the best decision I ever made.

But even if God doesn't give us our desires, that's okay, because He has something better in mind. Fictional Aaron King and real-life Jackie Stef can both fully attest to that.

Please stop by my Facebook page, Jackie Stef's Plain & Fancy, for book news and to view my Amish Country photography. I would love to hear from you!

Blessings and Peace,
Jackie Stef